Glitterella

Glitterella

Let it Shine

TRICIA GREENWOOD

HeartSpeak Publishing

DEDICATION

For the dreamers, the singers, the quiet stars...

This is your reminder that your magic matters.

Just the way you are. For those who hear music in the

wind and kindness in the silence, may your heart

always lead the way.

CONTENTS

PART TWO
The Castle of Light

CHAPTER ONE

The Spark Within

Long before the lights and the crowds, before her name shimmered across the world like a song, Glitterella was simply a girl with a dream, a journal, and a pen. At the farthest edge of the Wishing Woods, where moss grew silver in the shadows and the wind hummed like a lullaby, her story quietly began.

Her cottage stood at the end of a winding path, and hardly anyone traveled that way unless they were lost or meant to find her. Its windows sparkled even on cloudy days, and its roof sometimes caught the moonlight just right, shimmering like a waterfall. It looked as if it had been carved from starlight itself, wrapped in glass, and set down where the woods dared to end.

Inside, Glitterella lived tucked away from the world. Her name wasn't a stage name or a nickname; it was who she was. A name, her mother said, she was given in a dream for her before she was born. A name the world would one day know. But her mother was gone now, and Glitterella kept her shimmer mostly to herself.

She often paused by a narrow door in the hall, its frosted pane dim with dust. The music room had been locked since she could remember. Sometimes she thought she heard a faint note slip from behind the door, low and trembling, as though the silence itself was restless.

She did not go to school like other girls her age. She studied at home, with many books she loved, with her notebooks, and the quiet company of beautiful hummingbirds. Her favorite books to read were old volumes from the late 1800s and early 1900s, books of mainly philosophy, psychology, and religion, where she underlined quotes about love, courage, and truth, as she tried to understand how people's hearts and belief systems worked. Her days drifted by in slippers and soft robes, her desk scattered with pens and stacked journals.

She filled them with songs and stories, doodles and dreams, and sometimes her art, along with thoughts too fragile to say aloud. Most people didn't know she even existed. That never really bothered her much. She liked the peace she felt in the stillness. She liked being exactly as she was.

And yet... somewhere deep inside, she longed to be seen, for who she was, and for the part of her that lit up when she sang.

Every morning, she sat at the tall arched window of her bedroom, sipping her lemon tea with honey while bluebirds lined the fence as if waiting for her song.

Sometimes she sang softly. Sometimes she was brave enough to sing out loud.

That morning, she reached for her journal. The one thing in her world that felt truly magical. She hadn't written in days, not since dreaming that she was standing on a stage made of clouds, shining without fear. No lights. No cameras. Just her and the stars.

She opened to a clean page.

Wish #1: I want to be brave enough to sing out loud and touch people's hearts with my words.

Her pen lingered. Then the lyrics began to flow, so quickly that it was as if they were writing themselves. In the corner of her vision, tiny golden sparks flickered across the page, glowing faintly before vanishing into the paper. She froze, her breath caught. She knew what they meant.

Her mother's voice returned in memory: "Your gift is not like others. It was given from above, and it lives in the songs you write, in the words that shine from your heart."

Glitterella had made herself a promise: She would only write songs to heal, to comfort, and to set free. It was only for awakening the light hidden within their own hearts. Each spark was a reminder of that vow.

She bent back over the page.

Wish #2: I want to be seen for who I am and for my gift.

The golden sparks shimmered again, like a confirmation that she was on the right track in her life. Glitterella smiled through a rush of nerves. Sometimes she wondered if her songs might one day reach those who could truly hear them, not just as music, but as truth and healing.

She closed the journal softly, ran her fingers across the cover, and in that moment, the wind changed.

It swept through the cottage like a whisper on a mission, rustling pages, brushing her hair from her face, stirring the chimes into one clear, ringing note. Glitterella turned toward the window.

And there, on the sill, rested a tiny envelope. Silver-edged. Her name is written in flowing script.

Glitterella.

She could hardly breathe as she reached for it with trembling hands. The moment her fingers touched it, the paper pulsed with a faint golden glow.

Whatever was inside was meant for her.

And somehow, she already knew nothing would ever be the same once she opened it.

CHAPTER TWO

The Sound That Shimmered

The envelope balanced lightly on her lap, her name gleaming across it as if the ink itself carried music. Glitterella traced her finger across the letters of her name, afraid they might vanish if she blinked.

Inside on a small white card were ten words:

"Your heart holds music the world needs... Don't wait. Sing."

No name. No return address. Only a truth that felt both impossible and familiar.

She herself had written those very words in her journal once. The letter wasn't just a message. It was a mirror.

The air shifted. A glow stirred in her heart, as though the sparks from her journal had slipped quietly into her veins.

She crossed the room to the old keyboard beneath her window. Dust lifted as she opened the lid, the familiar scent of wood and time rising like a memory. She hadn't played in weeks, not since the night her voice broke mid-song, and she convinced herself no one would ever want to hear it.

Her fingers trembled on the keys. One note. Then another.

The melody returned like an old friend. She began to hum, soft as a secret, and the sound threaded into the night.

She knew it wasn't only memory that stirred the notes. Something greater was happening inside when she sang, a light she felt but never named. It was hers to carry quietly, a gift from above she dared not share... not yet.

"It felt as though the music itself had come down to meet her, as if heaven were lending her the strength and inspiration to play. Each note carried more than sound; it carried a spark meant to open hearts."

Above her, the chandelier stirred. A single crystal trembled, glowing faintly in rhythm with her voice. Once. Twice. Like a hidden heartbeat.

She stopped, startled. Silence fell. The crystal stilled.

Her heart raced, but this time it wasn't fear. It was recognition. Her music wasn't empty. It was alive. It shimmered.

She lifted the letter again and whispered the words: *Don't wait. Sing.*

It wasn't encouragement. It was permission.

No, more than that. It was a summons.

That night, she sat by her window long after the moon climbed high, brilliant and full. She didn't sing again. Not yet. But she was no longer afraid to be heard.

Tomorrow, she decided, she would sing in the Grove.

.

CHAPTER THREE
A Stage of Her Own

Glitterella rose before the sun, pulled on her favorite hoodie and soft leggings, and opened her journal.

She wrote, "Build a stage. "She thought, even if no one sees it but me. Her heart raced as she hurried into the yard. The air was cool and sharp, dew clinging to the grass like tiny diamonds. Behind the cottage, the Grove opened wide, its branches bending toward the light.

She gathered what she had: a few old boards stacked by the shed, last winter's string lights, and a handful of garden lanterns. Piece by piece, she shaped them into a little square stage, uneven but solid. She tied the lanterns to the low branches and strung the lights across them, humming yesterday's melody under her breath.

By midday, it was ready, a stage made of scraps and hope.

"It's enough," she whispered. "It's mine."

She put down a large rug and set up her keyboard, plugged in the cable, and checked the speaker for sound after running a long orange extension cord from the cottage to the stage. A microphone and stand were ready to go.

Everything worked. Her palms were damp. She thought to herself... this is so wonderful.

She closed her eyes and placed her hands on the keys. The first note rose into the Grove. Birds quieted. Leaves drifted down like applause. Glitterella's voice grew stronger, weaving light between the trees.

For the first time in her life, she felt truly seen, by the woods themselves, with the trees leaning in close to listen to her.

And she realized the bravest stage of all was not the one in front of thousands.

It was the one she built for herself, where the Grove was her only audience, and she sang beautifully.

Just before she stepped down, a single golden spark shimmered faintly across her journal resting nearby, then vanished, a quiet reminder that courage and her love for music and writing were bound together.

CHAPTER FOUR
The First Invitation

.·˙·. 🎵 .·˙·.

It had been two days since Glitterella's song had drifted through the Grove, yet its echo lingered like a secret glow. She leafed through the notebooks lined across her bookshelf, rereading words she once wrote and yet she thought were too fragile to share. She opened her journal, but the golden flecks that had shimmered around her felt too delicate just yet to be trapped in ink. It almost felt like starlight slipping through her hands.

But something inside her had shifted.
She sensed it in her steps, in the quiet way her breath moved. She walked taller, lighter, as though a hidden radiance had taken root within her, steady and waiting.

That afternoon, she opened her laptop and clicked through a few music apps she sometimes browsed for inspiration. Her internet presence was almost nonexistent, just a private account with small clips she rarely shared. They usually sat unwatched.

But not today.
Her eyes caught on the number beside her latest post. Three views. She blinked, leaned closer. Three.

It was only a thirty-second melody, recorded in the clearing and uploaded without a title, without expectation.
Her heart flickered. Could it be… someone had listened?

Then she saw it, an email notification, glowing at the top of her inbox like a tiny lighthouse.

Subject: Invitation to Perform, Maple Glen Community Fair

Her stomach flipped. She clicked it to open.

Dear Glitterella,

My daughter came across your music online and shared it with me. Your voice has such a warm, honest tone, and we were deeply moved by your song, even on that short clip we heard.

We'd love to invite you to perform a short set at the Maple Glen Community Fair this Saturday afternoon. It's a local event, very low pressure! Just a few neighborhood families, a small stage, and lots of homemade lemonade. Nothing fancy.

If you're interested, we'd be honored to have you join the lineup.

Kindly,

Miriam Lennox

Fair Coordinator

Glitterella stared at the screen for a long time.

"This can't be real," she thought.

She checked the address on maps online. Maple Glen was only thirty minutes away; she'd been there once with her Aunt Betty June years ago to buy fresh honey and tiny painted marbles. But now... she was being invited?

She closed her laptop quickly and paced her room. Her brain scrambled to make sense of the moment.

She wasn't ready. She didn't have more than two full songs. And the video from the clearing reminded her: maybe her voice is enough.

She sat on her bed and pulled her journal onto her lap. The page from a few days ago stared back at her:

Wish #1: I want to be brave enough to sing out loud.

Wish #2: I want to be seen for who I really am. These... were both being answered.

She took a breath and opened her laptop again. Her hands shook a little as she typed.

Hi Miriam,

Thank you so much. It'll be my first time performing in front of people, and I only have a couple of songs for a short set.

I'll be there.

With gratitude,

Glitterella

She hit send before she could change her mind. And for the first time in a long time, she didn't just feel like just a girl with sparkles and dreams.

She felt like someone becoming something.

As she closed her laptop, her journal on the desk quivered faintly. For an instant, golden threads shimmered across the words of her earlier wishes, as if the universe itself had whispered back: Yes.

She called Aunt Bette June, Glitterella's favorite grown-up, a bright-eyed, big-hearted aunt who hummed while she cooked and believed that every problem could be lightened with a little laughter and a song. Her kitchen always smelled like angel food cake that she baked regularly, and her stories shimmered with the kind of wisdom that comes from love. Aunt Bette June is the one who reminded her that true magic begins inside the heart.

The sun rose early on the morning of the fair. Glitterella had barely slept. She'd gone over her songs a hundred times in her head.

She'd tried on every outfit she owned twice. She'd even attempted to talk herself out of it. But the invitation she had printed out, now taped to her mirror, stood out like a quiet promise as she read it out loud:

"We'd love to invite you to perform..."
She couldn't back down now.

She chose a soft blue dress over leggings and her favorite denim jacket with rhinestones on the collar, just enough sparkle to feel like her, and her black boots. She loosely braided her hair. Her hands trembled as she packed her keyboard and a folded music stand into the back seat of her Aunt Betty June's car, who had driven over to pick her up from Meadowridge, a quiet town an hour away, where she lived in a small yellow cottage surrounded by wildflowers and wind chimes.

She had always been the kind of aunt who remembered birthdays, mailed glittery cards, and made everything feel like a celebration.

When Glitterella had called her late the night before, her voice shaking with nerves, asking if she could take her to the Festival of Maple Glen. Without a pause,

Aunt Betty June had said, "Of course, honey. I'll be there first thing in the morning." She was more like a second mom ever since Glitterella was little, someone who showed up, who listened without rushing, and who always believed in her sparkle, even when she didn't see it herself.

Sometimes, Glitterella wondered if Aunt Betty June carried secrets, too, or answers she would like to know. Once, when Glitterella asked why the music room stayed locked,

Aunt Betty June only smiled sadly and said, "Some doors take longer to open, sweetheart. You'll understand one day." The words had lived in Glitterella's heart ever since, like a question she was too afraid to ask again.

They were close enough and had their traditions, like singing together in the car to CDs of Frank Sinatra or the radio and stopping for coffee drinks and fresh donuts. Sometimes they made up stories about what they saw in the shapes in the clouds. It was only natural that Aunt Betty June would be the one to take her to her first performance.

They were almost there.

"You ready, sweetheart?" she asked with a sideways smile.

Glitterella nodded, clutching the small charm Aunt Betty June had given her before they left. It was shaped like a star, warm in her palm.

"As ready as I'll ever be," she said slowly...

"Are you sure you're, okay?"

Glitterella nodded quickly. "Yes. I mean... no. I mean, yes, I want to do this. I'm just... scared."

Aunt Betty June smiled gently and leaned over to squeeze her hand.

"Sweetheart," Aunt Betty June said softly, "Fear and gratitude can't live in the same room. Choose gratitude, and fear will have to leave. Have no worries, your guardian angel is always with you."

Glitterella glanced out the window, watching the trees blur past. Maybe her guardian angel would show up tonight, maybe in the lyrics, maybe in the lights. She didn't know. But somehow, Aunt Betty June's words made it all feel possible, as her soft hum filled the car along with her tapping the steering wheel to the rhythm of the song. She was humming a memorable tune that Glitterella used to sing as a child.

She almost welled up with tears of gratitude for her aunt's presence in her life.

Stepping out of the car at the festival felt great. It smelled like kettle corn and fresh-cut grass.

Aunt Betty June gave her a long, caring hug.

"I'll be right out front in the crowd, I'm your biggest fan," she said.

Glitterella gave her a big smile.

Kids ran between booths with painted cheeks and balloon animals. Parents sipped lemonade and browsed handmade jewelry. On the far side of the field, a small wooden stage stood beneath a canopy of twinkling lights.

It was simple. But real.

The volunteer at the sign-in table welcomed her with a clipboard and a warm smile.

"You must be Glitterella!

We're so happy you're here. You're slotted for the early afternoon set right after the folk duo and before the pie contest."

Glitterella blinked. "Okay."

Pie contest. Folk duo. Her.

This was happening.

She set up quietly at the side of the stage, fingers fumbling with cables and cords to be ready when her time came. She sang her songs in her mind again: The first was soft and familiar.

The second was her favorite. The third... well, she thought, "I'll do a cover song I know".

A little while later, her name was called.

"Please welcome today, performing for the first time...Glitterella!"

Applause rose gently, and she stepped onto the stage.

The sky was bright. The air was warm. Everything buzzed with color and life. Glitterella's palms were damp as she adjusted the mic.

She sat at her keyboard and paused. All the doubts returned like a wave. She thought, "What if they don't like my songs? What if I forget the words? What if my voice shakes?

She looked out at the crowd and saw a girl in the front row. Maybe nine years old. With freckles. And her hair was in a messy bun. Nervous eyes locked onto hers.

The girl mouthed one word: Hi.

Glitterella smiled back at her, and then she played. Her voice came out smaller than it did in her bedroom, or the Grove... and her hands almost played the wrong chord. But she didn't stop.

Halfway through the first verse, she saw the girl start to smile. Then nod. Then sway a little to the music, and everything seemed right. That was all it took.

The music no longer felt like hers alone. It belonged to the moment, to the child's smile, to the quiet magic humming between them.

"She realized her songs were never only her own. They were gifts flowing through her, meant to reach into hidden places and point every heart toward the One who first gave music its power."

By the time Glitterella reached the chorus, she wasn't thinking anymore. She was feeling. The way she always did when she was alone in the clearing. The song flowed

like it had always been waiting to be heard. She finished
to a warm applause, not wild, but genuine. And the girl in
the front row was clapping the hardest. Glitterella stood
and gave a little bow. She hadn't been perfect. But she
had followed through, and that meant everything.

CHAPTER FIVE

A Brighter Spotlight

"By the time Glitterella stepped off the stage, her legs felt light, almost as if the ground no longer held her. Her heartbeat in bright, steady waves, carried her forward on a joy within that felt endless, as though she were still performing."

"Sweetheart, that was beautiful," Aunt Betty June said, pulling her into a hug, "You didn't just sing; you connected with everyone listening. Did you see that little girl in the front row?"

Glitterella nodded. "Yes, I did. It was like the song was speaking right to her."

After the set, she wandered the fair like a ghost, quiet, invisible, watching everyone as if through a dream.

Later that evening, Glitterella sat on her bed with her laptop open and a half-sandwich in her hand.

Looking in her email, she hadn't even thought about checking online, and when she did...

The video of her performance at the fair was already posted.

A short clip. Thirty-seven seconds.

Titled simply:

"Local Girl at Maple Glen Fair with a Magical Voice."

The thumbnail showed her mid-song, eyes closed, bathed in soft golden light.

She clicked on it, and her own voice floated back through her external computer speakers.

She couldn't breathe for a second.

The caption underneath read:

"This girl didn't just sing, she just made us feel something.
We need more voices like hers."

There were already twenty-seven likes.

And another comment,

I was there. She made me cry a little.
What's her name? Glitterella? Love that.
More please.

Glitterella stared at the screen. It wasn't viral. It wasn't blowing up. But that didn't matter. It was something.

Some people had heard her.

And more than that, someone had felt her music.

Days later, as she clicked open her email. A new message glowed at the top.

Subject: Music Mentorship Opportunity, Rising Voices Collective

She blinked and read.

Dear Glitterella,

A colleague forwarded us your performance from the Maple Glen Fair. We were moved by your tone and presence. We're currently accepting submissions for a youth mentorship program focused on emerging singer-songwriters who use music to inspire change and connection.

Would you be open to a conversation?

Kindly,
Michaela James
Creative Director, Rising Voices

Glitterella put the laptop down.

She didn't squeal. She didn't jump up and down.

She just sat there. Breathing. How could this happen so fast? This wasn't a dream. It was a doorway.

And for the first time, the path ahead didn't feel impossible. It felt open.

It felt inviting. She glanced at her keyboard across the room. Just because it was inside her.

And she finally understood: the spotlight doesn't have to be blinding. Sometimes, it's just a light you learn to step into.

The Grove behind Glitterella's cottage had always felt like a secret, the kind that made your breath slow down and your heart soften. The type of place that felt like it whispered back to you when you were very still and quiet.

The trees stood like old friends in a wide circle, their leaves rustling in tones softer than words. Sunlight trickled through the branches in golden threads, catching in the tall grass and turning the air into something that shimmered.

Time didn't seem to follow its usual rules here. Everything felt peaceful. Everything listened.

She used to come here as a little girl with her mother, hand in hand, barefoot in the moss. They never needed to say much. Her mother would hum little melodies, half lullaby, half prayer, and Glitterella would close her eyes and try to catch them in her heart like butterflies.

This was before she knew what dreams cost. Before she knew that sometimes people leave, even when you need them most. Before she understood how quiet sadness could be, how it could sit beside you without saying a word and still fill the whole sky.

But back then, in this Grove, there was only wonder. You could hear the birds' songs and the wind. And love, unspoken, that wrapped around her like a soft shawl.

Even now, standing there alone, she could almost feel her mother's presence, the way she tilted her head to listen to the trees, the way her fingers tapped gently on Glitterella's shoulder in rhythm to a song only they knew.

That morning, Glitterella returned carrying her keyboard, a folding stool, and her journal, tucked under her arm.

She came to write.

She set up on the stage she built. The air smelled like moss and eucalyptus. She sat down, let her fingers drift across the keyboard, and didn't play anything. Not yet. She opened her journal and flipped past the lists, the to-dos, and the growing dreams. Then she found a blank page and wrote three words at the top:

For the girl I used to be.

She stared at them. She thought about that version of herself, the one who used to sit in this very same spot, pretending that her Beanie Babies were her audience and that she was brave enough to sing to them.

She imagined what she would say to that younger Glitterella now. She would tell her, "You're not too soft. You're not too much. Your voice matters, even if it shakes sometimes."

She began to play.

The chords were gentle and steady, like footsteps on soft ground. The melody formed slowly, built from fragments of old lullabies, heartbeats, and truth.

And then she sang.

Her voice carried through the branches, warm and golden, and something in the forest responded. A single leaf fell, spinning slowly. A bird chirped once, then went quiet. The world listened.

For a heartbeat, she wanted to speak it aloud, the truth of where her song's light came from. But the words caught in her throat. How could she explain that every note was borrowed, not born? That it was a gift whispered down from above, meant to awaken hearts?

Instead, she let the forest keep her secret, the music fading back into silence. The lyrics told a story, not of a girl trying to be something she wasn't, but of a girl finally allowing herself to be what she was all along.

"I don't need crowns, I don't need signs,
I carry my light from the inside.
I used to hide it. Now I see,
That every spark starts with me."

When she finished, she sat in silence for a long time. Glitterella packed up slowly, her heart full and steady.

She didn't record the song. She didn't even write down the lyrics. Because some songs aren't meant to be captured.

Some songs are meant to be felt and remembered forever.

CHAPTER SIX

A Song Worth Sharing

Two days after her time in the Grove, Glitterella sat on her bedroom floor with her laptop open, staring at the blinking cursor in a new message draft.

Subject: Re: Rising Voices Collective Mentorship Opportunity

She had typed

"Thank you so much for reaching out," and then no thoughtful words came... nothing.

Because she didn't know what to say.

She wanted to be brave.

But something about saying yes felt heavier than it should.

What if she said yes and they didn't like her songs? What if she said yes and tried to change her? Before she could overthink it again, she noticed a second email had come in the day before.

Glitterella opened it cautiously. Now, this one was from a woman named Avery Lennox, an independent music producer who had seen the same fair video.

Hey Glitterella,

My name's Avery. I work with young artists building their first EPs and developing their sound for digital platforms.

I watched your clip from Maple Glen, and I see huge potential. I'd love to connect about shaping your style into something more polished and current, maybe with a modern beat, a little remix energy?

I think we could elevate what you're doing and build something commercial and fresh.

Let's talk!

Avery

She understood what Avery meant. They wanted her voice, but maybe not her. She closed her laptop. Then reopened it. Then closed it again.

It was confusing, having people interested in her for the very thing she'd once kept hidden... and now wondering if they only liked the version they could reshape.

That evening, Glitterella sat on the window ledge, her guitar resting against her knees. She didn't play it often. The keyboard was her usual companion, but the guitar felt more personal somehow, like a friend you call when your heart is too full for words.

She played the latest song again on her guitar.

And while the melody floated into the fading light, a thought settled quietly in her heart:

It's not about being seen. It's about being true.

She didn't want to become someone else to make people listen. She just wanted to keep singing her songs that meant something to her, first, and let them ripple outward from there.

The next morning, she replied to both emails.

To Avery, she wrote:

Thank you for reaching out. I'm honored, but I think I need to keep finding my own voice before shaping it into someone else's version of success.

And to Michaela from Rising Voices, she wrote:

Yes. I'd love to talk. I'm still learning who I am as an artist, but I think that's the kind of journey worth mentoring.

She hit send, and this time, it felt right.

Because Glitterella knew the difference now.

A song worth sharing wasn't the one that made people clap the loudest.

It was the one that echoed in their hearts long after the last note faded.

CHAPTER SEVEN

The School of Sparkle

The invitation came on a Tuesday afternoon, this time, not from a festival or a producer, but from a fifth-grade teacher named Ms. Fern. Her email was short and simple.

Dear Glitterella,

I teach a small creative expression class at Riverbend Elementary, and one of my students brought in a printed photo of you from the Maple Glen performance. She said, "She sings like she means it."

A lot of the kids in my class are still learning how to feel brave enough to speak in public, let alone perform. Would you consider visiting our classroom? Nothing fancy. Just you, your story, and maybe a song

With hope,

Ms. Fern

Glitterella read the email three times before responding and picturing the whole vision in her mind.

She didn't hesitate another minute. She said yes.

It felt different than preparing for a stage. There would be no spotlight. No carefully timed song set. No microphones or festival energy. Just a small classroom, a group of kids, and her.

She packed lightly: her keyboard, a short playlist of her songs, a few sparkly stickers, and her original journal, the one with all the earliest lyrics and wishes.

When she arrived at Riverbend Elementary, Ms. Fern greeted her with a handshake and wide, grateful eyes. "You have no idea how much this means," she whispered.

Glitterella peeked inside the room.

She counted nine students sitting in a circle on a large, round carpet with moons and stars. Some sat cross-legged, others sprawled like tired cats. All of them looked curious and a little guarded.

Until a girl in the back stood up.

It was the same girl from the Maple Glen fair, the girl with the two messy buns and the freckled cheeks.

Glitterella's heart jumped. The girl gave her a rather shy, tiny wave.

It felt like coming full circle.

"Hi," Glitterella said gently, stepping inside. She pulled up a chair close to them all, sitting and said,

"I'm not here to just share a song, I also want to share a little bit of what I've learned about making writing lyrics to my music, about fear, and about being a quiet kind of brave."

The class was still.

She sat on the edge of her chair and told them about her cottage and about the letter she found on her windowsill. About the garden stage, and the first time she posted a video, even though her hands were shaking.

She held up her journal.

"This," she said, "is where I put all the things I was too afraid to say out loud. And now, those words are becoming songs."

Ms. Fern nodded slowly, as if she already knew.

One boy raised his hand. "Do you ever mess up and forget a word or a chord?"

Glitterella smiled.

"Sometimes, but only once on stage. But I've learned to keep on going and not react or make a face when I have, because most people don't connect to perfection. They connect to honesty."

Another student, a quiet girl near the window, said, "How do you sing when you're scared?" "You sing anyway," Glitterella answered. "You don't wait to feel brave.

You just do it... You show up. That's the magic."

"So... now, how would you all like to write some words to a song together?"

The class looked around at one another, nodded slowly at first, then all at once agreed with smiles.

She handed out mini journals and colored pens. On the board, she wrote:

What's something inside you that wants to be heard?

One by one, they wrote.

Some short lines. Some doodles. One boy simply drew a heart with headphones around it.

And then Glitterella sat at the keyboard.

"Ok, so now I am going to turn all your words poetically into a song."

A few kids looked wide-eyed, and the freckled girl smiled with glee and whispered, "Please, that would be so great."

Glitterella began to adjust the pages torn out from their journals and added their lines to her page and play.

Her fingers found a gentle melody, and her voice rose soft and clear, weaving their words into verses, one about hope, one about fear, one about dreaming even when no one cares. The room was silent by the end. And then, clapping.

Ms. Fern wiped her eyes.

"You didn't just visit us," she said softly. "You gave them permission to be creative in their own way."

Glitterella smiled.

That day, she walked back into her cottage carrying more than just her keyboard.

She carried something invisible but unmistakable: Proof that even the quietest voices can unlock something in someone else.

Not every song has to go viral.

Some songs needed to be sung in small rooms... for hearts that hadn't bloomed yet.

And those might be the most important songs of all.

CHAPTER EIGHT

A Golden Heart

The letter was in a plain white envelope, no glitter, no silver script, no return address.

Just her name, written in uneven pencil across the front:

To: Glitterella...

She found it tucked between her music sheets one morning. She had no idea how it got there. Maybe one of the Riverbend students had quietly slipped it into her bag. Either way, it found its way to her hands.

She sat at her desk and opened it carefully.

Inside was a folded piece of notebook paper, torn from a spiral pad. The creases were worn, as if it had been opened and closed many times before someone found the courage to send it.

Dear Glitterella,

My name is Sadie. I'm ten.

I heard your song in Ms. Fern's class.
I didn't say anything that day because I don't usually talk in front of people. But when you played my words in your song, I wanted to cry, but not in a bad way.

I felt like someone understood.

I lost my mom last year. Since then, I stopped singing. I used to sing all the time.

But when you told us that we didn't have to be perfect, and that being scared doesn't mean you're weak... I went home and sang to my dog.

I think my mom would have liked your music.

29

Thank you for helping me feel like my heart isn't broken forever.

Your new friend,
Sadie

Glitterella didn't move.

She read it again, slower this time. Her fingers trembled.

She thought about her mom, about all the days since she'd been gone. The quiet grief. The empty chair at the piano. The notes she hadn't sung. The words she had only dared to whisper into her journal.

She closed her journal and leaned back against her pillows, the chandelier above her catching the moonlight in its crystals. The glass shimmered faintly, a flicker like breath. She had felt her mother's presence that way before, as if the light itself remembered her. The thought frightened her almost as much as it comforted her. If her mother was still out there, why hadn't she come back? Glitterella turned onto her side, clutching the journal to her heart. The question glowed inside her, unanswered, as the night pressed close.

This letter wasn't just a thank-you.

It was a mirror.

It reflected something to Glitterella she hadn't seen clearly until now: her music didn't just brighten moods; it held space for pain. It permitted people to feel things they'd kept locked away.

It was a golden thread, weaving through hearts and memories, connecting one spark to another.

She gently placed the letter inside her journal and closed the cover.

Then she walked to the piano and lifted the lid. The keys were slightly dusty. Her breath caught as she pressed the first note, soft, familiar, like the beginning of a memory.

She played the melody she'd written in the Grove, but this time she added something new, Sadie's words. Her story. Her courage.

The music felt warmer. Deeper.

It was no longer just her voice in the song.

It was all the quiet hearts that had ever felt invisible. Every person who had whispered into the dark and wondered if someone, somewhere, might understand them.

That night, Glitterella recorded the song. No filters. No edits. Just her voice. With her hands on the keyboard.

She uploaded it with a title that felt right:

"For the Ones Who Don't Feel Seen"

And she signed it:

With love,

Glitterella

Then she lit a candle in the window.

Because some hearts need a light to find their way home

The morning after she posted

"For the Ones Who Don't Feel Seen,"

Glitterella went for a long walk. The Grove was alive with early sunlight and birdsong, and the path felt like it was humming beneath her feet. When she returned home, her inbox was full. She sat on the edge of her bed. Her fingers tapped to open the first message. "My sister showed me your song. I played it for my daughter. She's been quiet since we moved. Today, she asked to learn

piano." Glitterella blinked slowly, her heart rising with something soft. "I played your song while walking to school.
I didn't feel invisible today." "My brother's been in the hospital.
Your voice helped me not cry in front of him." I always skip talent shows.
But after hearing you, I signed up.
Just wanted you to know." Your song made me feel like I could be soft and strong."

"My mom heard me playing your song in my room. We talked for the first time in days."

"I write songs, but I never show anyone. You made me want to try."

"Thank you for being brave.
It helped me be brave, too."
She scrolled slowly, quietly. Each message felt like a light turning on somewhere in the world. Small, maybe. But real.

Glitterella leaned back, pulling her knees to her heart.
This... This was why she wrote songs.
To feel less alone.
And to help someone else feel that too.

There were dozens. All of them reaching back with the same message: You made me feel like I mattered.
She sat in her room for a long time, just reading.
She hadn't expected this.
Her music was becoming a mirror for others, the way Sadie's letter had been for her.
It wasn't just about singing anymore.
It was about creating a space, tiny but safe, where people could breathe, where they didn't have to shout to be heard. That afternoon, she opened a new page in her journal and wrote:

Project: The Sparkle Within
What if everyone had a journal? What if everyone wrote a line of something true, and then shared it in whatever way felt right?
What if sparkle didn't mean glitter and shine, but truth?
A truth that glowed in the dark.
A truth that helped someone else find their own within.

The idea wouldn't leave her.

By sunset, Glitterella had created a downloadable, printable document on her website. It was simple: a journal template with the words at the top:

"Write something you've never said out loud. Then choose:
Sing it. Share it... Sparkle... it forward."

Then she asked people to send in just one line they'd written, if they wanted. The next morning, they did.

A young teenager in Wisconsin wrote:

"I'm strong, even when I cry in the bathroom sometimes between classes."

A young boy in Portugal wrote:

"I still sleep with my stuffed animal because it reminds me of my grandpa, who gave it to me."

A mother of three wrote:

"I haven't danced in years, but your music made my feet remember how."

By the end of the week, her quiet little song had grown into something bigger than she could explain.

Teachers printed her journal pages.
Hospitals downloaded her music for teen therapy programs. One library added a Sparkle Station with colored pencils and a mailbox for anonymous notes.

And still, Glitterella stayed the same.
She sang at her piano.
She wrote songs about real feelings, real hearts, real people.

Not everyone would understand. Not everyone would like it. But the ripples were already moving outward. She didn't need to take them. She just needed to keep dropping the stone.

CHAPTER NINE

The Fear Returns

The invitation came in the form of a phone call. Glitterella had just finished steeping a fresh mug of tea when her phone buzzed on the kitchen counter. The caller ID read: Michaela James...

She wiped her hands on a towel, took a breath, and answered," Hello..."

"Hi, Glitterella!

It's Michaela, from Rising Voices Collective." came the warm voice on the other end of the line.

"I hope I'm not catching you at a bad time."

"No, not at all," Glitterella replied, steadying her voice even as her pulse picked up.

"I'll keep this brief," Michaela continued. "We've been following the response to your latest song and your Shine Within Journal. What you're doing is remarkable. And... we'd love to invite you to perform at the National Young Artists Summit next month."

Glitterella's heart skipped. Wow, could this be real?

The summit... She knew about it; it was huge. A national stage. A spotlight filled with nerves and lights and pressure. It was streamed around the world.

Speakers. Artists. Thousands of people.

Michaela's voice was warm.

"We'd like you to be the last performer on the second day. You can sing any song you want. No costumes, no changes, just you, the way you are."

There was a pause. Glitterella swallowed hard.

For a second, fear brushed against her. But then, something steadier rose to meet it.

She remembered what someone had written: "Thank you for helping me see mine."

Her voice came out quiet, but sure.

"I'd be honored," she said.

There was a soft exhale on the other end of the line, relief, maybe even joy.

"Wonderful." What's your email address?

As Glitterella shared her email address, her heart was racing... thinking she was finally ready to share herself.

"We'll follow up with the details soon. Thank you, Glitterella. This will mean more than you know." They said their goodbyes, and this time, Glitterella really heard it.

She hung up and set the phone down gently on the table, as if it carried something fragile. Then she sat back in her chair, hands resting quietly in her lap. The kitchen was still. She looked around the room and out the window, staring at the wind in the trees.

She had said yes, and her heart, once racing, now felt calm, anchored by something deeper than confidence.
It was a kind of knowing. A soft, inner certainty.
Like a seed that had waited long enough and was finally beginning to push through the soil. She wrapped her fingers around the warm mug of lemon tea, closed her eyes, and breathed in the moment. This wasn't the beginning of her dream.
It was the part where she stopped hiding it. The morning was quiet, heavy with fog. Glitterella sat on her bed, still in her robe, the covers unmade behind her, and yesterday's journal page still blank on the desk. She hadn't

touched her keyboard in three days. Even the butterflies outside her window seemed to flutter more slowly, like the world was waiting for her to decide.

The invitation to the National Young Artists Summit showed up in her email with details for the show.

"We'd love to have you close the second day..."

She closed her eyes.

She thought of Sadie, the girl from the letter. She thought of the quiet students at Riverbend Elementary. She thought of the forest, of her mother's piano, of her first written wishes.

And then, slowly, she stood.

She walked across the room and turned to face the tall mirror by her dresser, the one she rarely looked in. Not because she didn't like what she saw... but because she wasn't always sure who she was supposed to be.

Today, she didn't style her hair or put on sparkle gloss. She stood in front of the mirror and looked herself in the eyes.

And then she asked herself, out loud:

"Who are you doing this for?"

She pressed her palms against the mirror, and for a fleeting moment, she swore she saw a shimmer of gold behind her reflection.

It wasn't just her voice trembling now; it was the vow she had made to herself long ago. To use her gift only for good. To write songs that healed.

She would step into the light as herself, nothing more, nothing less.

Her voice was soft but steady. She walked over to her mirror and said out loud to herself...

"For the girl who's afraid no one will ever understand her."

"For the boy who hides his drawings in his backpack."

"For the kid who's never been applauded but still dares to try to perform." "And... for me.

She placed her hand over her heart. Felt her own heartbeat.

"I started this to be seen," she thought, "but I'll keep going to help others feel seen and heard." It seemed like some of the fear was still there. But now it had just a shadow. And shadows don't last when the light shows up. She recorded it in one take. And sent it to Michaela with a short note:

"I'm in. I'll close the second day.
And I'm bringing this song to share.

Thank you for making space for voices like mine."
– Glitterella

She stared at the message for only a second before clicking send...

Then she leaned back, her heart beating fast, not from fear, but from certainty. She walked to the keyboard and sat down. She didn't even need to warm up. The music came easily.

The melody was something new, built from all the softest notes of the last few months. It wasn't grand or showy. It was honest. Full. Like a diary entry turned into sound.

She added these words...

"I don't need perfect; I just need true."

CHAPTER TEN
The Performance

The days that followed were quiet but full. Glitterella rehearsed her songs gently, not only to perfect them, but to feel them in her heart. She sipped tea, scribbled lyrics in the margins of her journal, and walked through the Grove behind her cottage. Each night, she reminded herself: Show up and give it your all... just as you are.

By the time her suitcase was packed and zipped up, she felt something she hadn't expected: a calming peace.

The morning of the Summit had arrived with a pale, golden sky. Glitterella called for a cab, the driver tipping his cap as he loaded her case. The ride to the train station passed in silence except for the steady hum of tires on the road. She kept her journal open on her lap, tracing words with her finger like they might steady her heart.

The train carried her through fields and towns, gathering speed toward the city. As the skyline appeared in the distance, tall, gleaming, alive, her pulse leapt. She tightened her grip on the letter of invitation. This was real.

At the concert hall, she was ushered backstage. The space smelled faintly of polish and electricity, the air buzzing with nerves and tuning instruments. She stepped into the green room to warm up, but when she opened her mouth, nothing came. No notes. Just silence.

Her throat wasn't sore. Her breath was strong. But her voice had vanished.

Her hands trembled. She flipped through her journal, searching for comfort, but even her own words felt distant. Panic rose.

Michaela found her pacing and introduced herself... "I can't sing," Glitterella whispered.

Michaela placed her hands gently on her shoulders. "Take a breath and let's get you something warm to drink. Maybe your voice is waiting for your heart to catch up."

Glitterella closed her eyes and smiled. She thought of her mirror at home, of the question she had asked herself: Who are you doing this for?

A memory surfaced, her mother humming lullabies, brushing her hair, reminding her that music was never about being flawless. It was about being present. About sharing her love. She placed her hand over her heart. "I still have a song," she whispered. "Even if it's a quiet one."

A vibration stirred in her throat. A note. Then another. Raw, but real.

Hours later, her name was called.

She stepped onto the stage, and the lights were warm. The audience hushed. As she began to sing, her voice had returned; it was vulnerable, yet alive, and honest.

Every note seemed to echo farther than the walls of the hall. By the final chord, the room was utterly still. Then came the eruption: applause that rose, swelled, and turned into a standing ovation.

Backstage, Michaela embraced her. "You didn't just perform," she said. "You reminded them of what it means to be human with those lyrics."

Glitterella could only smile through tears of gratitude. Words weren't needed.

Later, in the lobby, a girl no older than ten with her mother stopped her, holding a notebook clutched to her chest.

"I don't talk much at school," she said softly. "But... I wrote something because of you. I think I'll sing it tomorrow. Just to my baby sister. But that still counts, right?"

Glitterella knelt on one knee close to her, smiling. "Yes, that counts."

The next morning, Glitterella caught a cab to the train station. The city shimmered in the early light, full of noise and promise. But inside, she felt calm. She boarded the train home, watching as the skyline slipped away.

By the time she reached the Grove, the evening had returned her cottage to its quiet glow. She set her suitcase down by the door, unlocked the door, and stepped inside. She pulled her journal from her satchel and wrote only one line:

I showed up. I let them see and hear me. And the world didn't close in. It opened.

She closed the notebook, her heart steady, looking around her home, she had brought something back with her: proof that courage doesn't always roar. Sometimes it whispers. Sometimes it sings.

And sometimes, that's enough to change everything.

"The Sparkle Within"

She let out a long, deep breath and looked up towards heaven with gratitude. Her keyboard sat where it always had, tucked beneath the arched window. Her journal was still open on her desk beside a dried flower she'd forgotten to press.

It felt so good to be back home. It was time to clean and organize things that had been overlooked.

A week later, as Glitterella was making her way over to sit down at the piano and write a new song, a few notes floated into the air, soft and searching, when the doorbell rang.

She thought... Who could that be? Usually, the mailman just left letters in the mailbox and continued his route. But today, he was standing right there on the porch, holding a thick bundle of envelopes wrapped with two rubber bands. His cheeks were pink from the breeze, and his eyes twinkled behind round glasses.

"Looks like many parts of the world have been writing to you," he said with a grin. "Must be something very special." She thanked him, her hands instinctively cradling the bundle like something delicate.

As she stepped back inside, she closed the door gently behind her, heart thudding in quiet wonder.

After the summit, Glitterella had uploaded a free printable version of her "Shine Within Journal" on her website, along with her address for fan mail...with one simple invitation printed on the cover in silver script:

"Write something honest and poetic you've never said out loud to anyone."

She had meant for the journal to be a gift. Now, seated at her table, she carefully slid the rubber bands off and placed the stack in front of her. Twenty-seven letters. Each envelope was different. Some were drawn with stars; others were smudged with fingerprints or stickers.

They came from everywhere: New York, Brazil, the Philippines, Iceland, and a small town called Eagle, which she'd never heard of in Idaho.

Her fingers trembled as she opened the first one. It was written on a printed page from the journal, which she had offered online.

"I've never told anyone I'm scared of being forgotten."

The second:

"I want to be strong, but I sing and sometimes cry in the shower when I cannot sing in key, so no one hears me."

Then:

"Sometimes I feel like I'm too much. Or not enough. I don't know which."

Letter after letter unfolded like petals, honest, raw, and beautifully human

"My brother passed away last year. I miss him most when music is playing.

"I love to dance, but I hide it. No one knows who I am when I'm alone."

"I'm eleven. I wrote a song last night. It was about stars, and how they don't leave even when it's cloudy and we can't see them."

She held the letters and notes over her heart for a moment; her breath caught somewhere between awe and ache.

These weren't just fans. These were souls. Brave enough to whisper truth to the page and somehow trust her to receive it. A few of them included photos, little doodles, on folded paper. One had cut out a heart shape from glittery red construction paper and taped it inside their letter with the words: "Thank you for helping me see mine."

Tears welled up.

This wasn't applause.

This was a connection.

This was why the music mattered.

She placed the open letters in a circle around her on the floor, like a halo of voices, and began gently replying; most of them included their email address. She worked on one note at a time.

She then finished unpacking her suitcases, placing her journal beside her bed, and inserting the folded program from her performance into the back pocket of her journal.

Then she read her last entry in her journal,

I want to be seen for who I really am.

She smiled. Not because the wish had magically come true. But she dared to act on it when the opportunity came.

She wasn't trying to fit into a version of herself that sounded louder, shinier, or easier to explain.

She had her own rhythm now. Her own glow. And it came from within.

The next morning, she woke up with a song on her mind, a song for just herself.

She sat at her keyboard and played the first few notes. Then she paused. She didn't need to rush.

There was no deadline or pressure. Just a melody, and now she finally knew what it meant to sparkle without asking for approval first.

She flipped open a fresh page in her journal and began to write.

"I used to think the magic lived in the moment.
But it was always living in me."

She set the pencil down, exhaled softly, and gazed out the window. Thoughts drifted and circled, tugging at her like melodies she hadn't finished.

Were her words enough? Would anyone hear her song?

Maybe they would. Maybe they wouldn't. Either way, she'd keep singing.

She lifted the pencil again and let the words spill across the page:

Sometimes the world doesn't need another star on a stage, she wrote.

"It needs a brave heart, one that reaches out with kindness, sings with compassion, and writes songs to lift and heal. A heart that reminds us of we already shine; we just need to share the love inside us by being who we truly are and singing what's real."

CHAPTER ELEVEN

Let It Shine

.·˙·. 🎵 .·˙·.

It started as a hum. A quiet tune that found her one morning while she was brushing her hair.

No piano. No guitar. Just a rhythm in her heart and mind and a line that wouldn't leave.

"So let the light in... It's time...let it shine

She sang once.

Then again.

Then grabbed her journal and wrote it down.

It didn't feel like the other songs. This one didn't whisper. It glowed, bright and bold.

She sat at her keyboard and let it build. Verse by verse. Layer by layer.

A heartbeat song, with a chorus full of courage and light.

Verse 1

I used to sing in the shadows,
Sometimes all alone in the dark.
Hiding every melody
That flickered in my heart.
I never thought I'd really try,
No one even knew my name...
But the spark inside was burning bright,
And calling me to fame.

Chorus

Let the light in, let it grow,
You don't have to sparkle just for show.
Every quiet dream you keep,

Can rise like stars from where you sleep.
So let the light in...
it's time
Let it Shine

Verse 2
I felt like more than just a whisper,
In a world so loud and fast,
But magic doesn't rush its bloom,
It grows until it lasts.
It's not fame, not gold, not glory,
But a feeling deep in my chest
That when you share your love and story,
You help someone else feel blessed, -

[Bridge]
This song is for the quiet hearts,
The ones still finding where to start.
You're not too small, you're not too late,
You're made to love and create

Final Chorus
Let the light in, let it shine,
In your own rhythm, your own time.
You don't have to chase the crowd,
Just be yourself and sing out loud.
You were never meant to hide,
The glow you've carried deep inside.
So let the light in...
Let the light in, let it shine,
let it shine,
Let the light in, let it shine,

By the end of the day, she had something real. Something big. Something that felt like the sun finally rising inside her.

She titled it *"Let It Shine."*

She looked for a recording studio in town and hired an engineer named Robert, who owned his studio there, to help her record her song.

A music producer who worked with the studio, named Stephen, said he could hear more instruments for her song and said he would like to work on it if she would like him to. Glitterella agreed that it would be amazing to add more instruments.

A week later, Robert called her to come into the studio to hear what he and Stephen had produced with all the instrumentation, and Glitterella went in to listen to her song and loved it, bringing tears to her eyes; they all agreed, it was a beautiful song.

She took a copy of it on a thumb drive home with her and played her new song on her speakers, and then she videotaped herself singing along with it and uploaded the video online that night.

Glitterella woke to her phone buzzing nonstop.

She sat up, her heart pounding, and scrolled. Texts. Emails. Messages from a couple of people she hadn't heard from in years, but mostly from people she didn't know. Her song had exploded overnight. Not just views, thousands of them.

"I love your song."
"I cried in my car in the parking lot."
"She's the voice of this moment."

It wasn't just her city, or even her country. People from all over the world were listening.

Someone in Brazil had written: *"I don't understand every word, but I feel it."*
A nurse in Toronto shared: *"I played this in the ICU last night. My patients smiled."*
A girl in Japan wrote: *"This song gave me the courage to want to sing to my class."*

Glitterella pressed a hand to her mouth, eyes stinging. Her song, the one she had written, had crossed oceans. The Grove was still outside her window, still dewy and hushed, while her phone pulsed with the noise of the world. The contrast made her chest ache.

Then she saw the headline.
A well-known pop blogger had posted:
"Glitterella isn't chasing stardom. She's creating a new kind of light. 'Let It Shine' is honest, powerful, and joyfully polished. A glittering song of belonging."

Belonging. The very thing she had once thought was out of reach.

Her phone buzzed again. This time it wasn't a text or a tag, it was a call from a number she didn't know. She hesitated, then answered.

"Glitterella?" The voice was warm, confident, with the kind of calm that carried authority. "This is Mara Stone, director of the Global Heartbeat Tour."

Glitterella's pulse spiked. She had read about the tour, a worldwide music charity bringing artists together for uplifting performances in cities across the globe.

"I wanted to tell you," Mara continued, "your song reached us. We've never seen a response quite like this. We'd love to invite you to join the tour this summer."

Glitterella swallowed hard. "Me? On… on the tour?"

"In London," Mara said. "On a real stage, with your name glowing across the screens."

Glitterella's breath caught. London.

"But there's more." Mara paused, as if weighing her words. "We want you to close the show. The final act always carries the message we hope audiences take home in their hearts. 'Let It Shine' is exactly that message."

For a long moment, Glitterella couldn't speak. She glanced at her worn keyboard in the corner, at the journals stacked by her bed. It didn't seem possible that the same girl who once whispered wishes into the wind was now being asked to carry the closing song for a global stage in London.

Her heartbeat raced as she agreed to be there, and gratitude steadied her. Gratitude for the Grove, for the song that had found her, for every trembling moment that had carried her here.

Mara's voice softened. "Good. The world is ready for your light, Glitterella. We'll be in touch with the details."

The call ended. Glitterella sat frozen, her phone clutched in her hand. The silence in her room felt enormous, as though it was holding its breath right alongside her.

Slowly, she lay back against her pillow, staring at the ceiling as her heart pounded in her chest. She reached for her journal and wrote one trembling line:

The world has listened. Now I must answer.

She closed the book, pressed her palm against the cover, and whispered into the quiet: *When the time comes, I'll be ready to step forward.*

CHAPTER TWELVE
Rockstar Rising

Weeks blurred into a rush of rehearsals, paperwork, and sleepless nights that spun past like lanterns in the wind. The call had turned into a ticket, and the ticket had carried her across the sea. And now, Glitterella was here, backstage in London.

The weight of Mara Stone's words still echoed in her mind: "The world is ready for your light."

The air backstage buzzed with nerves and electricity. She passed other artists pacing, water bottles in hand, their voices warming up in quick bursts. Technicians whispered into headsets. A low hum pulsed beneath her boots, the vibration of tens of thousands waiting.

Her name, GLITTERELLA, glowed in soft gold across the giant screens. The sound of the crowd swelled like a wave gathering strength. For the first time, she felt what it meant to step not just onto a stage, but into a destiny.

She smoothed her jewel-bright pants, chosen not because they were fashionable but because they felt like her. No stylists. No compromises. Just Glitterella.

The stage manager gave her a nod. The music swelled.

She stepped into the glow.

The jewel-encrusted keyboard shimmered before her. She touched the mic, closed her eyes, and whispered, "Thank you."

Then she placed her fingers on the keys and began to sing:

"Let the light in, let it grow,
You don't have to sparkle just for show.
Every quiet dream you keep,
Can rise like stars from where you sleep.
So let the light in… it's time… let it shine."

The crowd erupted.

Her voice rose, and with it, her story. Behind her, a video montage filled the giant screens, children in classrooms singing her lyrics, fans holding up journals, stars sparking across the sky in rhythm with the song.

Phone lights swayed like constellations, tens of thousands of tiny lanterns rising in the dark. Glitterella's breath caught. For a heartbeat, it looked as if the night sky itself had bent down into the arena to sing with her. By the final chorus, the whole arena was singing with her.

Not in perfect pitch. But in unity.

"Let the light in, let it shine,
In your own rhythm, your own time.
You don't have to chase the crowd,
Just be yourself and sing out loud.
You were never meant to hide,
The glow you've carried deep inside.
So let the light in…
Let the light in, let it shine,
let it shine,
Let the light in, let it shine."

She threw her arms wide, lifted her mic high, and let the sound roll like thunder made of hope.

The lights dimmed. A single spotlight followed her.

For a breathless moment, the arena was utterly still. Glitterella could hear her own heartbeat, feel the warmth of every gaze locked on her. The silence didn't feel empty, it felt full, like the world was holding its breath with her.

And in that one moment, she wasn't just Glitterella, the girl from the Grove.
She was Glitterella the Rockstar.

But even more than that, she was the voice of everyone who had ever been afraid to sing, and somehow a new fearless feeling was growing inside her.

The stage lights had faded; the tour posters were put away. The viral videos had slowed. But the music inside Glitterella hadn't stopped.
She had sung on one of the world's largest stages, and yet when the noise finally quieted, her heart
whispered: "Remember why you started."

After London, after Let It Shine circled the globe, after the interviews and applause and glittering magazine features… Glitterella decided she needed to figure out the next steps.

She went home, not because she was tired, though she was, but because she was overwhelmed. She knew that if she wanted to keep shining, she had to stay rooted in why she had started.

The crystal cottage welcomed her like an old friend. The trees swayed softly outside her window.

She didn't open her laptop or check her messages… She opened her journal and on a clean page, she wrote:

Fame fades, spotlights dim. But hearts remember. I don't want to be a star that people stare at.
I want to be a light that helps them see themselves.

That night, she had an idea…

Not a tour or another album. But maybe a movement.

She was thinking about it as she fell asleep, and when she woke up in the morning, she decided it would be called The Shine Sessions.

Instead of giant stadiums and sold-out arenas, she would visit places that rarely saw music up close:

- Children's hospitals
- Foster homes
- Rural schools
- Youth shelters

She brought with her an acoustic guitar, her journal, a portable speaker with a microphone, and a suitcase full of sparkly-star notebooks to hand out to some younger attendees. She also brought her phone with a tripod to record them all singing. On her journey to all the different places she traveled to, she was touched by many people, young and older.

In one classroom, a shy boy named Luca wrote in the notebook Glitterella gave him:

"I don't talk in groups. But I dream in songs."

In a hospital room in Seattle, a girl with braids and an IV wrote:

"I want to be strong like you and sing like your voice."

Glitterella turned those lines into songs.

She sang them with the kids and recorded them on her phone.

Later that evening, after uploading a new Shine Session, Glitterella curled up with her laptop to check her email for messages. Families had written to thank her for the way their kids had enjoyed their time with her. Teachers shared stories of students growing braver in class. Each note warmed her, but one message stood out, stopping her scrolling hand.

From: Caleb R.
Your Shine Sessions reminded me why I started playing guitar in the first place. If you ever want someone to join you in music, I'd be honored to be the one to perform your songs with you someday.

Glitterella read the lines twice, then again. Her pulse quickened. She didn't know this person, not really, yet something about the name shimmered on the screen. Caleb. It almost glowed there like a note waiting to be struck, like a thread she couldn't yet see the other end of.

She leaned back, the soft light from the screen painting her face in silver blue. Around her, the cottage was still. Outside, the Grove whispered in the wind, as if listening too.

She whispered the name under her breath. Caleb. It felt familiar in a way she couldn't explain, almost like the echo of a melody she had once dreamed of but never played.

For a long moment, she let the message sit open, her heart caught between hesitation and possibility. Then she smiled, small but certain, and whispered to herself:

Maybe... someday we will meet in person.

CHAPTER THIRTEEN
A Letter to Herself

The sky was soft with early lavender light.

Glitterella sat curled on her windowsill, the same place she had once whispered her first wish into the wind. A cup of her favorite lemon tea steamed beside her. She loved lemon tea with honey because it warmed her throat, a habit she had learned from one of her vocal instructors she admired.

Her journal lay open, but she hadn't written in days. She'd been thinking about how she used to be so afraid to sing in front of people because of a childhood experience that had her bound deep within.

But now she finally understood that "FEAR" stands for False Evidence Appearing Real, and in that moment, she felt the weight lift, realizing most of what had held her back was only make-believe. She reached for her favorite pen and wrote a letter to herself, for the kind of girl she used to be, one who might need the words she wished someone had given her.

Dear …,

I remember what it was like to sit quietly while the world hurried past, wondering if my voice would ever matter. I used to sing only to myself in the silence, pretending that was enough, yet secretly hoping someone might hear. Not for fame, but for understanding. For the chance to be seen as I truly was.

Here is what I've learned: I don't have to be flawless to be loved. But I do need to open my heart, choose kindness, and let forgiveness make more space for love. No one is perfect. And that's where grace lives.

Because faith, truth, and light are the treasures only we can give when we allow them to come through us from above. And the world doesn't need them someday. It needs them now.

I will write the words. Sing the songs. Share the piece of myself I once thought too fragile to show. Because somewhere, someone is waiting for it. And when they hear it, they'll remember they can shine their own light, too.

Fear cannot stand where gratitude lives. Choose gratitude, and your light will always find its way through.

With all my heart,
Glitterella

That night, she slipped the letter into a separate notebook titled The Next Chapter, to be passed on to the next heart that needed it.

Blowing out the lanterns, she let her song echo quietly in her heart. She whispered a promise to herself: when the time came, she would step forward.

In that moment, she understood what she wished every heart could know: being a rock star was never about glitter or spotlights. It was about courage, gratitude, and sharing your truth so others can remember theirs.

And maybe that was the real secret: you don't need a stage to shine. You only need the faith to let your own light be seen.

Outside, the night held its breath around her. And though she didn't know it yet, somewhere across the

ocean, a boy with a guitar named Caleb was already
writing one of his own.

If a voice can cross the silence, maybe it can find me,
too.
If a song can light the darkness, I'll follow where it leads,
to you.

Two songs, born in different worlds, are already part
of the same melody.

Dawn arrived soft and gray, a pale mist of light
spilling across her windowpane like a sigh. Glitterella
stirred from the wide windowsill where she had drifted
into a shallow sleep, her cheek pressed against her open
journal. The pages smelled faintly of ink and lavender, her
last written words blurred by the damp air.

On the desk nearby, the letter waited. Its cream
envelope, now creased at the edges, carried no return
address, only a wax seal embossed with a treble clef and
the words Prague Conservatory of Music.

When she first opened it the week before, her breath
had caught halfway between disbelief and wonder.
A scholarship. A full invitation.
An opening that hadn't existed a week ago.
And chosen...somehow, her.

No one had written her name on a waiting list. No
one had told her to apply. The letter had simply arrived.
Slipped beneath her door, the official seal glimmered like
truth, and the printed words left no room for
doubt: Your talent has been recognized. Your place
awaits.

Her suitcase stood by the door, polished silver
latches catching the faint morning light. The lavender
blanket, her aunt had given her lay folded on top, lace

edges soft from years of washing. She brushed her hand over it, tracing each thread like a goodbye.

Before the car arrived, she laced up her boots and stepped outside. The cold bit gently at her cheeks. Mist curled low over the path, coiling between the trees like breath. The Grove seemed to hold its own kind of silence that morning, not empty, but watchful, like an old friend refusing to say farewell too loudly.

She followed the trail past the mossy stones and stopped at the crooked stage. The wooden boards sighed under her weight as she set her keyboard case down. Her fingers slid along the railing where she had once whispered wishes into the wind, those fragile confessions that had seemed to vanish in the dark. But now, she thought, maybe the Grove had listened all along. Those whispered dreams had turned into lyrics. Those lyrics had become songs. And somehow, those songs had carried farther than she could ever see.

Still, her voice trembled as she whispered, "I'm a little terrified."

A crow called in the distance, its cry echoing through the branches like a reminder that every flight begins with a leap. Glitterella closed her eyes and drew in a deep breath, letting gratitude rise through her chest until it steadied her heartbeat. The fear didn't disappear, it softened, blending into something fierce and shimmering.

She turned back toward the cottage, gathered her suitcase, and met the driver waiting at the end of the lane. The tires crunched over gravel as the car pulled away, the Grove shrinking behind her with every turn.

At the airport, the world came rushing at her, bright signs flashing in strange languages, rolling suitcases thudding like distant drums, voices weaving together in a chorus of arrivals and departures. The ceilings arched overhead like cathedral domes, and the scent of coffee mingled with jet fuel. Everything felt too large, too alive.

She clutched her passport in one hand, the scholarship letter in the other, the paper trembling slightly between her fingers. She read the words again, even though she'd already memorized them. Full tuition. Immediate placement. Prague. Each line felt unreal, like reading a lyric she hadn't written yet. Her throat tightened.

CHAPTER FOURTEEN

The Conservatory

The air in Prague carried the scent of rain and fresh bread, warm, yeasty, and strangely sweet, curling through the narrow streets like a song the city hummed to itself. Bells tolled from unseen towers, their notes rolling across rooftops and into the morning haze.

Glitterella pressed her forehead to the taxi window as the driver steered through the maze of cobblestone lanes. Rain slicked the stones until they shone like glass, reflecting the glow of lanterns that still burned faintly though daylight had climbed across the sky. The city moved around her, umbrellas opening like blossoms, trams clattering past, voices lilting in languages she barely recognized.

She held her satchel close against her chest. Inside it, folded and smoothed until the creases nearly disappeared, was her scholarship letter, the single proof that she belonged to this new world of bridges, music, and strangers.

The car turned alongside the Vltava River. The water flowed wide and dark, carrying reflections of bridges and spires in rippling silver lines. Tourists leaned over the railings, laughing beneath umbrellas. Street musicians sheltered beneath awnings, coaxing melody from violins and accordions that sighed through the drizzle. The music wove through the air, tender and alive.

Her throat tightened. She thought of Aunt Bette June's kitchen window and the bluebirds that perched on the fence, of the Grove and its crooked stage wrapped now in mist. The lanterns strung along the Charles Bridge flickered in the gray light, reminding her of home, the kind of glow you only noticed when you were far away from it.

The taxi pulled to a stop before an immense building of pale stone. Rain traced thin lines down its carved façade. Massive oak doors loomed ahead, their panels inlaid with bronze music notes that gleamed even beneath the clouds. High above the entrance, words were etched deep into the stone:

Conservatorium Prague.

Her pulse thudded. This was it.

She stepped out into the chill, her boots striking the wet pavement. The scent of rain thickened. Students hurried past her, juggling instrument cases, notebooks, and umbrellas, their laughter echoing against the stone archways.

Glitterella lifted her face to the building, feeling small beneath its grandeur. Then, drawing a steadying breath, she crossed the threshold.

Inside, the Conservatory seemed to breathe. Music floated from every corridor, piano scales ascending like light, a cello humming deep and low, a voice lingering in the air so clear it felt almost holy. The marble floor mirrored chandeliers that dripped gold light across vaulted ceilings painted with fading murals of muses and winged figures holding lyres.

Her footsteps echoed as if she were walking through the inside of a heartbeat.

At the Registrar's desk, a woman with silver-rimmed glasses peered up from her paperwork. "Yes?" she asked in brisk, accented English.

Glitterella fumbled for the letter and handed it over with both hands. "I... I'm here on scholarship."

The woman scanned the page, nodded once, and stamped a form with a sharp click. "Welcome to the Prague Conservatory, Miss Glitterella," she said, sliding a folder across the counter. "Orientation, nine o'clock tomorrow. Here is your schedule, student identification, and a map. Explore if you wish, many do. But take care. It is easy to lose yourself here."

"Thank you," Glitterella murmured, her fingers trembling slightly as she accepted the papers.

The woman's eyes softened. "Don't be afraid of the echoes," she said quietly. "Every great musician leaves them behind. Let them be a reminder, you are not alone."

Glitterella blinked, warmth catching at the edges of her eyes. She nodded, clutching her folder to her chest as she stepped away.

The corridors unfolded like a maze; every hallway lined with portraits of composers whose eyes seemed to follow her. Doors opened to bursts of sound, violins tuning, pianos rumbling, laughter echoing up stairwells. She tried to follow the map, turning left, then right, but each passage looked the same.

Her pulse quickened. "Breathe," she whispered. "Just breathe."

She rounded a corner too quickly and collided with someone.

A guitar case slammed softly against the wall. Papers scattered across the polished floor like startled birds.

"I'm so sorry!" she gasped, dropping to her knees to help.

The boy crouched at the same moment. Their hands met over a page, fingertips brushing.

Across the sheet, a few lines of handwritten lyrics bled in uneven ink:

If a voice can cross the silence, maybe it can find me too.

If a song can light the darkness, I'll follow where it leads, to you.

Something inside her caught, an echo she already knew.

The boy lifted his head. His eyes, green with flecks of gold, widened with surprise. Then he smiled, hesitant and genuine. "I didn't think anyone else would ever read that," he said softly.

Glitterella's voice came out in a breath. "But I've already heard it."

He blinked, startled, then laughed, a quiet, disbelieving sound full of wonder. "I'm Caleb."

The name struck her like a chord she had once played. Caleb James.

His notebook still trembled in his hands, pages loose and rain spotted. He hadn't meant to drop it. Those words weren't finished yet, just fragments born from nights spent playing alone on the Charles Bridge, letting the wind carry melodies over the river. For weeks, he had written and wondered if anyone out there could hear him.

And now, impossibly, here she was.

He noticed her satchel, stuffed with loose pages, lyrics without music, words waiting for a home.

A spark steadied in him. He smiled again, this time sure of it. "You look like someone who's been carrying a song too."

Outside, the bells struck the hour. Music rose through the halls like breath.

For a heartbeat, the world around them faded, the corridors, the voices, even the river's sound. There were only two hearts, two notebooks, and one invisible thread humming between them, drawing them closer, measure by measure, toward the melody that would soon become theirs. Morning broke with church bells, dozens of them, ringing from spires across the city. The sound rolled like waves, some bright and playful, others solemn and deep, until the whole air shimmered with bronze.

Glitterella stood at the narrow window of her small guestroom, clutching her blanket around her shoulders. She had never heard so many bells at once. It was as if the city itself had woken singing.

Caleb waited downstairs, leaning against the stone arch of the doorway, guitar case slung over his shoulder. "Ready?" he asked, his grin warm but teasing.

"As ready as I'll ever be," she exhaled, fingers tightening around her journal tucked in her bag.

They walked through cobbled streets where bakeries spilled warm bread smells into the air and cafés brimmed with chatter in languages, she only half-understood. Musicians busked on corners, a violinist spinning a melody that made children laugh, an accordion spilling a tune so full of ache it felt like homesickness itself.

Glitterella slowed to listen, her heart torn between awe and doubt. So much music already lives here.

Caleb must have seen it in her eyes. "Don't compare," he said gently. "Every note has its place. Even the quiet ones."

The conservatory loomed at the end of the square, a grand old building of marble and glass, its steps worn smooth by centuries of students.

Gold letters gleamed above the tall wooden doors: Académie de Musique.

Inside, the halls echoed with sound. Pianos spilled scales behind heavy doors, voices rehearsed arias that rattled the windows, and cellos hummed like thunder rolling underfoot. Students hurried past with stacks of sheet music, faces intent, fingers stained with ink.

Caleb led her up a sweeping staircase into a rehearsal hall. High ceilings arched above, painted with faded frescoes of angels carrying trumpets. Rows of chairs circled the stage, each holding an instrument, waiting for hands.

"This is where I've been working," Caleb said softly, reverence in his voice. "And where you'll get your chance."

Glitterella set her keyboard down gingerly, as if afraid the old walls might reject it. She pressed a single note. It rang out, clear but small in the cavernous space.

"It sounds... too soft here. Like it'll disappear."

Caleb knelt beside her, strumming a chord that bloomed warm against the walls. "Then let me catch it." Together they played a simple melody. The acoustics carried their sound farther than either expected, wrapping it in velvet and sending it to the far corners of the hall. Caleb set his guitar down gently, eyes searching hers and said,

"It feels like more than music when we play. Like something else is woven into it."

She had never spoken about her gift, her truth, aloud before, not to her aunt, not to friends. But in this moment, his words unlocked the silence she had kept for so long.

"Because it isn't only me," she whispered.

"The shimmer in my songs comes from above. It's meant to open hearts, to let God's love through."

Caleb didn't look away. His expression steadied into wonder, not doubt.

"I believe you are someone chosen to bring more love into the world with your words and music. I felt it the first time you played. That's why it moves people so much. Because it carries more than just your voice."

A woman in a long coat entered abruptly, her heels clicking smartly. She paused, listened, then smiled. "You must be Glitterella. The woman studied her kindly. "I see that look of wonder in your eyes... every student asks themselves the question whether they belong, or whether they are willing to listen and learn. Europe has its songs. You must let them meet yours."

Then, with a nod, she swept away, her footsteps fading into the hall. Glitterella sat very still, her fingers pressed to the keys. She wasn't sure if the woman's words were a welcome or a challenge. Maybe both.

After rehearsal, Caleb walked her through the gardens behind the conservatory. Fountains splashed in marble basins, and roses climbed the trellises, spilling color into the afternoon air. He watched her quietly as she scribbled in her journal.

"What did you write?" he asked at last.

She read it aloud:

Wish #16: To let this city's bells, bridges, and voices weave into my song without drowning out my own.

Caleb smiled, "That's not a wish. That's already happening."

She laughed softly, but the doubt in her heart didn't vanish. It only shifted, softer now, like a question waiting for its answer. That evening, as they crossed the same stone bridge where they had reunited, the bells tolled again, scattering birds into the sky.

Glitterella leaned on the railing, watching their wings catch the fading light.

"Daunting, isn't it?" Caleb asked, leaning beside her.

"Yes," she admitted. "But also... inspiring. Like standing inside a song bigger than anything I've ever known."

"Then maybe it's time," he said gently, "to add your verse."

She glanced at him, her heart tight but steady. Maybe Europe wasn't about being louder. Maybe it was about daring to let her quiet voice join the choir of a city that had been singing for centuries.

And for the first time, the thought didn't frighten her. It thrilled her.

CHAPTER FIFTEEN

First Notes at the Conservatory

The conservatory air smelled faintly of resin and old wood, as though centuries of songs had seeped into the beams. Glitterella followed Caleb down the echoing hallway.

He walked easily, guitar case slung across his back. In the lantern-glow of the tall windows, his hair caught copper threads, and his smile calmed her even when the rest of her shook inside.

He wasn't polished like the students in pressed jackets and neat ties. He was warmth and earth, steady as his chords. And yes, handsome in a way that sometimes stole her breath when she wasn't ready for it. But handsome wasn't why she trusted him. It was the way he saw her, even when she faltered.

They entered the workshop room, a tall chamber with wide windows and rows of chairs already filled. Students tuned violins, scribbled notes, adjusted reeds. Glitterella clutched her journal, feeling small among the confident bustles.

At the front stood Maestro Rinaldi, silver-haired, broad-shouldered, and sharp-eyed, though his expression carried a faint smile. "Welcome," he said, his accent curling the vowels. "Today, we explore voice not as performance, but as presence. Music lives only when it is shared. Each of you will offer a fragment, anything. A scale, a song, even a hum. We will listen. We will learn."

One by one, students rose. A girl sang a crystalline aria that filled the rafters. A boy played a piano étude so quick it scattered like rain across glass. Applause followed each, polite but genuine.

Glitterella's stomach knotted tighter with every performance. I don't belong here. I'm too plain. Too soft. She pressed her journal against her heart like armor.

"Glitterella?" Maestro Rinaldi's voice broke into her thoughts. "Would you share something?"

Her knees trembled as she stood. Caleb gave her a small nod from the back as she turned to look at him, his steady eyes and gentle smile just enough to say, you can do this.

She set her keyboard on its stand, her fingers quivering on the keys. For a moment, silence pressed too heavily. Then she closed her eyes and whispered to herself: Even one note. Start there.

She began with a hum. Thin, quiet. She almost stopped, but the acoustics caught it, stretched it into the corners of the hall, and suddenly her note sounded fuller than she had imagined. She played a chord, added words without meaning to:

"If fear is the night,
I'll carry a star.
If home is a Grove,
I'll take it afar."

When she opened her eyes, the room was still. Students leaned forward, not in judgment but in attention. Maestro Rinaldi's sharp eyes softened further.

"That," he said quietly, "has presence."

Heat rushed into her cheeks. She bowed her head quickly, embarrassed by the sudden clapping rising around the room.

Caleb caught her eye as she returned to her seat.

Glitterella sometimes caught her classmates staring when she sang, as though they felt something more than music. They would blink, unsettled, then applaud too quickly, not knowing why. Her heartbeat quickened each time. She knew why. Her gift shimmered inside every note, tugging at feelings they hadn't meant to reveal.

And so, she learned to hold back, to round the edges of her songs so they sounded beautiful, but not too piercing. To dim her glow so her classmates wouldn't feel what they weren't ready to feel.

Caleb was different. When they played together, she sometimes felt almost a spiritual connection between them, her heart answering his chords before her mind even caught up.

After the session, Maestro Rinaldi approached her. "Your voice carries something rare," he said. "Keep it steady, and Europe will listen."

Glitterella hugged her journal close, her heart aching in the best way. For the first time since leaving the Grove, she thought: Maybe I do belong here. Even in this city of bells, my song has its place.

The workshop ended as the sun slipped behind the rooftops. Glitterella lingered by the doorway, still feeling the echo of her voice in the conservatory walls. She had half-expected to be invisible, but Maestro Rinaldi's words still warmed her heart.

Caleb appeared at her side, guitar slung across his back. "See?" he said softly, nudging her shoulder. "Told you."

She smiled, a little shy. "I thought my voice would vanish in there."

"Your voice could fill cathedrals," he said, then grinned, "and probably make half the pigeons fall off their ledges."

She laughed, the tension in her heart loosening. His jokes weren't flashy; they were easy, like a stone skipped across water. Behind them lived something steady, and she had come to rely on it.

They stepped out into the city. Streetlamps flickered awake one by one, halos of gold glowing on the cobblestones. The air smelled of rain and roasted chestnuts from a vendor closing shop.

Shadows stretched long across the bridges, while the bells tolled another hour, softer now, as if the city had lowered its voice for the night.

They walked in silence for a while, their footsteps syncing on the stones.

"You were incredible today," Caleb said at last. His tone was different now, not teasing, not playful, but sincere. "The whole room was excited to hear you. I've been here for weeks, and I've never seen that happen."

Glitterella shook her head. "I was terrified."

"Good." He glanced at her, his expression open. "It means you cared enough to let them in. Most people just try to impress."

His words settled inside her like a lantern being lit. Yet her heart tightened too, because she knew what the others couldn't, that it hadn't only been her voice. It had been the shimmer of her secret, reaching into places she had vowed to touch gently. She prayed Caleb couldn't see it in her eyes.

They reached the river, its dark water carrying broken reflections of the streetlamps. Caleb leaned on the railing, and she stood beside him, hugging her journal.

"Back home," she said quietly, "I always had the Grove. The crooked stage, the lanterns, Aunt Betty June sometimes over, and baking in the kitchen. Here it's louder and sharper, I keep thinking I might lose myself."

"You won't." His voice was steady, certain. "Because the Grove isn't just a place. It's you. You carry it with you every time you sing."

She turned toward him, surprised by the depth of understanding in his eyes. In the lamplight, they looked warmer, brighter than she'd ever noticed. Handsome, yes, but more than that: safe.

Caleb exhaled, raking a hand through his hair. "Can I tell you something?

"I feel like I'm constantly trying to prove I deserve to be in the room. But when I play with you…" He hesitated, searching for the words.

"…I don't feel like I must prove anything. I just get to be me."

Glitterella's wanted to respond, but the words tangled with the secret she carried. So instead, she set her hand lightly on the railing, closer to his. Their fingers brushed, hesitated, then rested together, small and certain.

Neither spoke. They just watched the river flow, their shadows leaning into each other beneath the streetlamps.

Later, as they walked the last stretch toward her guesthouse, Caleb said softly, "Glitterella?"

"Yes?"

"I'm glad you came. Not just for the music. For...
everything."

Her heart swelled, tender and fierce. "Me too."

At the door, they parted with a lingering look,
neither needing to say more. The connection between
them glowed, steady as the lamps lining the quiet street.

The notice went up on the conservatory board one
misty morning:

Midwinter Showcase Auditions
Open Call for Vocalists.

The words shimmered on the page, daring anyone to
read them twice. Whispers rippled through the halls as
students gathered, eyes bright with hunger. For many,
this showcase was the chance of the season: a
performance in the great marble hall, streamed to patrons
across Europe, doors flung open to careers waiting just
beyond.

Glitterella stood in the circle of students, her heart
pounding. Caleb leaned close to her, his shoulder
brushing hers, his voice low.

"You should audition."

Her stomach clenched. "Caleb, I can't. These
students have been training for this their whole lives. I'll
look foolish."

His smile was gentle but firm. "You could never look
foolish; you'll look like yourself. That's all you've ever
needed."

A girl with a clipped bob and a silver lanyard glanced
over as they spoke, her eyes cool, assessing. "Everyone
auditions," she said to no one in particular. "Those who
belong rise. Those who don't... learn faster." Her gaze
slid past Glitterella as though she were made of air. A boy

beside her smirked, already humming an aria under his breath.

The day of auditions arrived. The marble hall echoed with nerves and ambition. Names were called one by one. Glitterella sat gripping her journal, while listening as powerful voices filled the chamber, operas soaring to the rafters, pop ballads that shook the windows, intricate harmonies delivered with dazzling control.

Her turn came at last.

She walked to the center of the stage, the stone floor cold beneath her shoes. The panel of judges waited in a long row, pens poised. Their silence weighed more than applause ever had.

Caleb stood at the side, guitar slung across his back. He gave her the smallest nod. She breathed in deep.

Her fingers trembled as she set them on the keys. The first note quivered in her throat, threatening to crack.

The judges' pens hovered.

She thought to herself...What if I fail here? What if they see me as too soft, too small?

She closed her eyes. The Grove rose like a photographic memory behind her lids, the crooked stage, lanterns glowing, Aunt Betty June humming in the kitchen.

Caleb's voice joined it in her mind: You carry it every time you sing.

She began softly, a hum that gathered courage as it rose. The melody unfurled like breath, steady and sure, her voice threading through the hall until it found its own wings.

Glitterella sang softly...

"When the world feels wide, and the night feels long, I lift a single light, and turn it into a song."

"When the rain won't end, and dreams drift far, I
follow the wind, to where the echoes are."

The melody deepened, her tone blooming from
tremor into warmth as she moved into a chorus that filled
the vaulted space:

"Cause even in the silence, I still hear you call,
Your voice moves through the shadows, steady through it
all.
Every piece I've lost still beats softly inside
I'm still here, still here... where I belong."

Her voice wove into the marble's echo. It wasn't
perfect. But it was hers.

The final note floated upward, fragile and luminous,
then fell into silence. A hush rippled through the rows.
One judge blinked hard, as if a memory had returned
unbidden. Another sat back, his pen forgotten, listening
not with his ears but with his whole being.

Glitterella sensed it, the faint shimmer inside the
sound, so she gently rounded the last phrase until it
settled like light on water.

By the time she finished, the hall was hushed. The
silence stretched, fragile and full. Then one of the judges,
the woman with the long coat who had once told
her, Europe has its songs; let them meet yours, leaned
forward and said simply:
"Presence."
A few judges were writing notes. One older judge nodded
to the others in agreement.
Relief swept through her heart so fast it left her dizzy.
She bowed, clutching her journal to her heart as she
stepped offstage.
Back in the wings, Caleb caught her in an embrace before

she could protest. "You did it."

"I don't know if I passed," she whispered into his ear.

"You don't need their yes to know you belong," he said. Her cheeks burned. She pulled back, flustered, but his eyes were too steady, too warm.

As they moved down the corridor, the girl with the silver lanyard stepped aside to let them pass, a smile that didn't quite reach her eyes.

That evening, when the results were posted, Glitterella found her name among the chosen. Her breath caught. She turned to Caleb, who was already grinning like he'd known all along.

The weight of it hit her then: She was part of the Conservatory now... and yet, as the bells rang in celebration overhead, her heart trembled, not from fear this time, but from the strange, powerful awareness that she was falling in love with everything she was experiencing.

Later, by the window, she opened her journal to capture the day. As her pen moved, a single fleck of gold pricked the margin, then quickly faded. Once, that spark had frightened her. Tonight, it felt like a vow-keeping time beneath her ribs. Gentle, always gentle, she promised, and closed the book.

CHAPTER SIXTEEN

A Song Between Them

The list of names for the Midwinter Showcase stayed pinned on the conservatory board all week, a beacon that made Glitterella's heart skip every time she walked past. Her name sat there, neat, official, undeniable.
She carried both pride and nerves in equal measure. It wasn't enough to be chosen. Now she had to deliver.

One evening, as the bells finished their last golden tolls, she and Caleb slipped into an empty practice room. "Golden light angled through the high panes, filling the silence with a soft warmth."
Caleb rested his guitar against his knee, the last chord still humming in the air. He gave a small, almost shy smile.

"I grew up in Brighton," he said, voice low, as if testing how much of himself to share. "My dad taught me guitar when I was little, and my mother played piano. Music was always in the house, and I always practiced diligently. Then I came here to Prague last year, hoping to learn and that this conservatory would help me to get even better."

Glitterella tilted her head, curious. "And has it? Do you feel like you've found what you were looking for?"

He laughed softly, a hint of frustration in it. "Most days, no. I feel like I'm chasing something just out of reach. Everyone here is brilliant, and I start thinking maybe I'll never be enough."

Her hands lingered on the piano keys. "You are enough. I could hear it in the way you played."

Caleb looked at her then, really looked, his hazel-green eyes steady. "But playing with you," he nodded toward the keys, "it doesn't feel out of reach anymore. It feels… real and true."

Glitterella's breath caught. No one had ever said that to her before.

"All right," he said. "We've got to come up with something for the showcase that's… us. Not just you. Not just me. Us."

Glitterella perched at the piano, her journal open on the stand. He leaned forward, his grin crooked, his hair falling into his eyes. "Glitterella, you know… together," he strummed a lazy chord that hummed warm against the quiet. "Together we're unstoppable."

They began with fragments. She played a soft progression, hesitating at the last note. Caleb caught it, smoothed it, turned it into something that circled back. She scribbled a lyric in her journal:

"Between the silence and the sound,
is where the heart is truly found."

He read it over her shoulder, his breath warm against her cheek. "That's it. That's the chorus."

They sang together, halting at first, then laughing when they stumbled. Each mistake became a thread that drew them closer. By the third try, their voices had found a braid, his low and steady, hers rising like light through leaves. A beautiful harmony.

The more they shaped it, the more she felt the pull, the familiar, golden tug that asked her to open the door wider. She eased it back, softened an interval, chose the honest note over the dazzling one. The song brightened anyway, as if it knew how to glow without being asked.

Hours passed unnoticed. Shadows crept across the floor. Their song grew, half hers, half his, yet somehow fully theirs.

Caleb leaned back at last, stretching his arms over his head. "You realize what we just did, right? We wrote our new song in one day."

Glitterella looked at him, her heart aching in a way she didn't have words for. His eyes caught the last light from the window, and in that moment, she saw him not just as her anchor, not just as her friend, but as something more. It was the warmth in his gaze, the way he saw her as if she were already enough, that made her breath catch.

She whispered, almost without meaning to, "Our song."

He smiled softly. "Yeah. Ours."

Silence fell again, but this time it wasn't heavy. It shimmered, full of possibility. Glitterella's hand drifted toward his on the piano bench. Their fingers brushed, lingered. Neither moved away.

Outside, the snow dusted the rooftops as the city prepared for its winter festival. The smell of roasted nuts and cinnamon filled the air. Children tugged mittens, dragging their parents toward carousels painted with faded horses.

The whole place shimmered as if the season itself had strung a necklace of lights across the streets. Glitterella and Caleb carried their instruments toward a small stage near the fountain.

"It's not the showcase," he said, grinning beneath his wool cap, "but it'll be good practice."

She smiled nervously, hugging her keyboard case. "Small stages feel bigger to me sometimes."

He nudged her shoulder. "Then let's make it ours."

They set up under the falling light snow, warming their fingers against cups of cocoa. A small crowd gathered, curious. Caleb strummed the first notes of their new song, and Glitterella followed with the piano. Their voices rose together, blending in a way that felt like fire against the cold.

> *"Between the silence and the sound,*
> *is where the heart is truly found.*
> *Build a bridge of light,*
> *from me to you,*
> *If you hold one end,*
> *I'll hold on too."*

The crowd leaned closer, bodies swaying as if the song itself pulled them nearer. A little boy high on his father's shoulders, clapped in rhythm, his mittened hands sparking joy with each beat. Warmth spread all through Glitterella, and for the first time in Europe, she felt she belonged to the music, to the city, and to this moment.

On the bridge behind her, the shimmer tilted toward something brighter. A woman pressed a hand over her heart, as though steadying emotions she hadn't expected. Nearby, a young man blinked hard, brushing at his eyes in surprise. Glitterella eased into the final chorus, letting it settle soft and weightless, like snow drifting onto stone. The glow lingered anyway.

When silence finally returned, the applause rushed in, spilling through the square in waves. She bent down to close the latches on her keyboard case and closed it, letting it rest behind her against a wall as she turned to the crowd. Where she met the gaze of a cute little girl, and she smiled. "Did you like it?" she asked her, her voice carrying the tender hum of the music. The girl nodded yes quickly, shy with her hands clasped beneath her chin as if holding the moment safe.

Glitterella was so taken by this little girl and... that was when it happened.

In a blur. A young guy, who couldn't have been more than seventeen years old, tall and wiry, with his hood pulled low over sharp cheekbones, lunged forward. His coat sagged at the seams, and before anyone could react, he yanked the keyboard case from behind Glitterella and bolted. Glitterella froze. Her hands still hovered where the keyboard had been. A hollow drop opened in her heart. "My keyboard,"

Caleb was already on the move... his guitar still on his back swung like a ballast as he cut through the crowd. The thief darted down the frozen stones, long legs sure despite the ice. He shoved through onlookers, nearly toppling a stall of paper stars. Caleb closed the distance, boots hammering the square. The boy slipped, caught himself, then swung the case like a shield when Caleb lunged.

They grappled, shoulder to shoulder, fists clenching fabric, the case between them. For a moment, it looked as if the boy might win. His eyes flashed in the lantern light, not cruel but desperate, like someone who had run out of choices.

"Not yours," Caleb yelled, loud and angry.

The boy wrenched free, vanished into the maze of faces and alleys, empty-handed. Gone.

Caleb stood, heart heaving, the case still in his grip. Around them, the festival hushed, whispers skimming over the square like falling snow.

She met him halfway. Her cheeks were bright with cold,

and she was in shock. "Caleb, you could have been," She didn't finish.

He pressed the case into her hands, grin crooked, breath clouding the air. "And let him walk off with your music? Not happening." Her throat closed. She wanted to argue, to hold him, both at once. Instead, softer than she meant: "Thank you."
Something in his look shifted. A grin turned to a vow. "Always."

For a beat, the square was hushed. Then someone in the crowd began to clap, slow and deliberate. Another joined, and soon the applause swelled again, different this time. Not just for the music, but for the courage they'd just witnessed. Lanterns shook as people waved, mittened hands rising high above the stalls.

Glitterella tightened her hold on the keyboard and glanced at Caleb. He nodded toward the edge of the square. Together they slipped away through the parting crowd, the cheers following like a winter wind, carrying them out into the night.

Snow drifted again, and for a while they walked in silence through the wet streets. The music still shimmered in her, but so did the memory of Caleb's hand gripping the case, his vow still echoing in her ears. For the first time since arriving, she felt Prague itself had taken notice of them, not just the songs, but the bond that carried them.

Once inside her room, she set the case on the rug and let her hand rest on the latches, a silent blessing for what had been lost and returned. When she lifted the lid, her journal lay waiting. She drew it out carefully, as if it, too, had survived a journey.

On a clean page, she wrote,

Thank you for keeping us safe.

Thank you, Caleb, for bringing me back my journal.

Even before the ink settled, a soft breath of gold unfurled across the margin, drifting like starlight caught on the page. It lingered longer this time, pulsing faintly, then dissolving into the paper as though the journal had whispered its own reply.

The room held its breath, charged with wonder, and she felt certain the gratitude had been heard.

CHAPTER SEVENTEEN

Shadows Before the Showcase

It struck her how quickly a night could change, from applause to panic, from having her journal and keyboard stolen to cheers that carried them home. She still felt the weight of Caleb's grip on the case, the vow in his eyes. That memory steadied her. But by morning, the city had already moved on, its voice rising for something new. The posters appeared overnight, pasted on walls, tacked to café doors, bright against the winter gray:

MIDWINTER SHOWCASE

Académie de Musique

Featuring: Voices of the New Generation

Every street seemed to echo it. Every bell seemed to toll for it. And every step Glitterella took through the conservatory halls carried the same refrain: this mattered. The Winter Festival had been chaos and joy, firelit and free. But this, this was marble columns, velvet seats, and cameras pointed straight at her. One wrong note here would echo for years.

At rehearsal, her fingers trembled. For a flash, she thought of the night before, how close she had come to losing her precious journal.

"Your song is… so delicate," one student murmured. "But will it carry?"

She smiled back, thin, rehearsed. Inside, the words sank like stones: Too soft. Too small.

The girl with the silver lanyard adjusted her music folder. "Audiences love a story," she said lightly. "But judges want technique." She turned away before

Glitterella could answer, as if the conversation were already finished. Why were these girls acting so petty, she thought...

That night, she sat in her room, staring at her closed journal. Usually, the wishes came easily. Tonight, nothing. Just silence.

A knock. Caleb eased in, hair tousled, guitar case leaning heavy against the wall. His grin was worn, but warm. "You disappeared after rehearsal. Everything okay?"

She almost lied. Instead, she shook her head. "What if I can't do it? What if I stand there and nothing comes out? What if they all see I don't belong?"

He crossed the room, dropped to a crouch before her. "You've already proved it. To the Grove. To Alder Creek. To me." His voice dipped. "You've lit up more people than you know, and if you forget, I'll remind you every time."

Her eyes watered. She tried to laugh it off. "You're too good to me."

He tilted his head, quiet for a moment. "Not good enough."

The words hung between them, heavier than air. His gaze didn't move. Neither did hers. For a moment, the whole room stilled.

Her pulse surged. Gratitude shifted, trust deepened, and she felt the truth rise, clear, terrifying, and undeniable. Love.

She broke first, fumbling for her journal. "I should get some sleep."

Caleb rose, but as he did, his hand lingered against hers;

the brush of his skin sent a current right through her, as though he'd spoken without words.

"Tomorrow," he said softly, his gaze holding hers. "Together."

Her pulse quickened. The warmth of his touch stayed with her, blooming into something she couldn't hide from herself anymore, something that felt like the beginning of more than a promise.

When the door closed behind him, she opened the journal at last.

Wish #17: To sing with love...

Doubt still circled like shadows. But in the center of them, a new flame sparked, one that had nothing to do with marble halls or critics.

Everything to do with Caleb.

Below, someone crossed the courtyard humming a tune she didn't know. As she listened, a thin line of gold seemed to hover along the journal's edge, no brighter than moon lace, then faded, leaving only the quiet and her steadying heart.

Snow fell in slow spirals on the night of the Midwinter Showcase, enough to blur the sharp edges of the city. The conservatory shimmered under golden banners and wreaths of evergreen; its great doors open wide as streams of people in wool coats and silk scarves hurried inside.

From the balcony windows, the marble hall glowed like a lighthouse. Its chandeliers sparkled with a thousand facets, each crystal catching the flicker of candles. Musicians tuned their strings, whispered scales, and adjusted sheet music beneath the vast painted ceiling. Backstage, Glitterella stood perfectly still, her fingers

clenched so tightly around her journal that the edges
bent. She could hear the murmur of hundreds beyond the
curtain, students, patrons, critics, strangers whose
opinions would be written in columns by morning.

Each voice outside pressed against her heart like a
weight. She turned a page in her journal, looking at the
line, she had written the night before.

"Glitterella."

She jumped. Caleb had slipped backstage, his guitar
already strapped across his chest, a quiet grin playing at
his lips. His hair was tousled as if he'd run a hand
through it a dozen times, but his eyes were steady, always
steady.

"You're shaking," he said gently.
"Because I'm terrified," she said with a shaky laugh. "I
don't know if I can do this."

He studied her for a long moment, then reached for
her hands. His palms were warm against her cold fingers.
Remember the Grove? You thought you were alone, but
the forest echoed back. You don't have to carry this alone
tonight, either. I'm right here... we're in this together."

Her breath caught. His closeness, his certainty, it was
almost too much, but it steadied her flame.
"You make it sound so simple," she whispered.
"It is," he said. "Sing because you love to. Sing because
the world needs it. The rest... the rest doesn't matter."

The call came: "Next, Glitterella and Caleb,
presenting an original piece."
Her heart lurched. The curtain drew back, revealing the
stage: vast, blinding beneath the chandeliers. Rows of
velvet seats stretched upward, filled with faces she

couldn't count. The silence of expectation weighed more than applause.

She stepped forward, and Caleb took his place beside her, with his guitar ready. She touched the piano keys, her journal open beside her like an anchor.

For a moment, her throat closed; the marble hall felt too large. Then she felt Caleb's presence, a beautiful chord humming low and warm as he strummed. She looked at him and saw, in his eyes, not judgment or pressure but love, quiet, certain, undeniable.

She drew a breath and let the first note out.

It quivered. It almost broke. But the marble caught it, lifted it, spun it into the rafters until it was no longer small. Caleb's guitar folded around it, steady as a heartbeat.

The melody grew. Her words rose.

> *"Between the silence and the sound,*
> *... is where the heart is truly found.*
> *Build a bridge of light,*
> *from me to you.*
> *If you hold one end,*
> *I'll hold on too."*

The hall stilled. People leaned forward. Her voice no longer felt like hers alone; it was woven with Caleb's, with the chords of his guitar, with every wish she had whispered into her journal since the Grove.

A critic in the third row lowered his pen. Glitterella felt the shimmer gather, so she gentled it, choosing the true note over the triumphant one. The sound warmed instead of blazing, an intimate presence felt even closer.

When the chorus came, something inside her shifted. She wasn't singing to impress. She wasn't singing to prove. She was singing because her heart had found its flame.

On the last note, silence wrapped the room in gold. For a heartbeat, it was as if the world held still, listening. Then the applause rose, stronger, louder, warmer than she had ever heard.

Glitterella's heart swelled with a rush of relief and wonder. Her song had carried. She had carried.
She turned to Caleb, and in the glow of chandeliers, with applause crashing like waves around them, she saw him as she never had before, his grin wide, his eyes bright, his whole being lit by pride and love. And she realized: she wasn't just singing with him. She was in love with him. Backstage, she collapsed against the wall, laughter and tears spilling at once.

Caleb caught her in an embrace, guitar bumping awkwardly between them.
"You did it," he whispered.

"We did it," and she laughed.
She pressed her forehead against his heart, listening to his heart pound as fiercely as hers. For the first time, she believed, not just in her voice, not just in her courage, but in them.

As they pulled apart, the journal slipped from her hands and opened to the wish. For a blink, a dusting of gold breathed across the page. Caleb's gaze flicked down; his breath caught. He didn't speak. He only laced his fingers through hers, steady as ever.

"Come on," he murmured, a smile in his voice. "Let's take our bow." The secret settled between them, like a promise waiting for the right time.

The applause still rang in her mind long after the curtains closed. Glitterella walked through the marble halls in a daze, Caleb's hand holding hers as they slipped out of the conservatory into the cold night.

Snow drifted down in lazy flakes, muffling the city's edges. Lanterns along the river burned low and golden, casting halos into the darkness. The noise of the crowd remained behind them; here, the world was hushed, as if holding its breath.

Glitterella pulled her coat tighter, her cheeks still warm from stage lights. She had never felt so exposed and so alive in the same moment. Her heart hummed with two truths: she had sung with courage, and she had sung with love.

But love was the harder truth.

They walked in silence at first, boots crunching on snow. Caleb glanced at her with a grin that wouldn't quite quit, his breath fogging in the air. "You were brilliant," he said. "The way the hall just... stopped for you? That's something I'll never forget."

Her throat tightened. She wanted to tell him she felt the same about him, about the way his beautiful guitar playing had wrapped around her voice. She wanted to confess that when she looked at him under the chandeliers, she hadn't just seen her partner. She had seen the boy she was falling in love with.

But the words in her heart felt scared. What if she said what she felt out loud, and he didn't feel the same? So instead, she laughed softly, trying to keep her voice steady. "We were brilliant. Together."

Caleb tilted his head, studying her as though he
heard what she wasn't saying. His smile softened.
"Together," he echoed.

They reached the stone bridge, snow gathering along
its railings. Caleb set down his guitar case and leaned
over, "You know," he said, voice lower now,

"I've played a lot of songs in a lot of places. But
nothing has ever felt like tonight. Not even close."
Glitterella hugged her journal with her heart pounding.
"Because of the hall? The showcase?"
He turned to her, eyes steady, shining in the lamplight.
"Because of you."

The words wrapped around her like warmth against
the cold. She could have stepped in closer then, could
have closed the space between them and let her heart
speak its truth. But what if this was just the afterglow of
success, a moment that would fade with the snow?
She looked away, blinking hard.

"I don't know what comes next," she whispered.
Caleb didn't press. He only reached out, brushing
snowflakes from her hair. "We'll figure it out," he said
quietly. "One song at a time."

A gust swept across the bridge, lifting a curl of paper
from the wet stones, a discarded program that fluttered
and spun, skipping past their boots before catching
against her journal. For an instant, the gilt letters on its
cover shimmered, as if holding something brighter than
lanternlight.

A thin breath of gold flickered along the edge, there,
then gone. Caleb's eyes followed it, his gaze lowering,
then lifting to hers with a softness that said everything he

didn't. She held the book close to her coat, her pulse ringing like a struck bell.

That night, alone in her small room beneath the slanted roof, Glitterella opened her journal. Her fingers trembled as she turned to a fresh page. The air smelled faintly of rain and candle wax. She pressed her pen down and wrote:

Wish #18: To be brave enough to love, even if it means risking my heart. She closed the book and lay awake, torn between wonder and fear, knowing she loved him, but not yet knowing if she dared let him know.

CHAPTER EIGHTEEN

A Winter Confession

The bells of Prague carried across the rooftops as Glitterella stepped out into the pale morning. She was out on an early walk to clear her thoughts when she nearly bumped into Caleb rounding a corner.

He steadied her, grabbing her hand, his smile quick and warm. "I was hoping I'd run into you."

Her pulse skipped. "Literally?"

"Best kind of luck," he said. Then, after a beat, they both cracked up.

"Breakfast? There's a café not far."

The little café smelled of coffee and cinnamon rolls, its windows fogged from the heat inside. They tucked themselves into a corner booth, coffee cups warming their hands. For a while, they spoke of light things, the oddness of hotel pillows, the sound of bells that seemed to mark every passing hour.

But soon, the talk deepened.

"You were awfully quiet last night," Caleb said gently. Glitterella hesitated, tracing the rim of her cup.

"I was… afraid of saying too much."

"Too much?"

She wanted to tell him right then and there: I love you. I'm terrified of losing you. Instead, she whispered, "Sometimes the things that matter most are the hardest to say."

He leaned closer, eyes steady.

"Then don't wait."

His smile flickered, vulnerable now. "

Glitterella, nothing I've played has ever felt like it did with you. It wasn't the building or the stage. It was us."

She smiled and winked at Caleb. After breakfast, they let the city guide their steps. As they crossed Charles Bridge, its stone saints watched from their ledges. Street musicians played under arches, violins weaving songs that echoed as she glanced at Caleb, and he was watching her, as if the music bound them in the same quiet spell.

They wandered into Old Town Square, where the Astronomical Clock chimed, its golden face spinning a dance of time. Tourists craned their necks, but Glitterella found herself watching Caleb instead, the wonder in his eyes brighter than the clock itself.

At St. Vitus Cathedral, they stood shoulder to shoulder beneath soaring arches, their silence full of reverence. Stained glass scattered color across the marble floor, and Glitterella felt the same light filtering through.

Later, in Lesser Town, they paused at the Lennon Wall, where layers of paint and words pressed together into a chorus of hope. Caleb reached out, brushing his fingers over a faded heart scrawled in red.

"Feels like everyone... too scared to say something, found a way here," he murmured.

The words she was feeling were still trapped inside her, yet the city seemed to whisper them back at her from every corner:

"Don't wait."

By the time they reached Kampa Park, lanterns glowed along the river, their reflections shimmering across the Vltava. Caleb stopped, snow catching in his hair. "This city's beautiful," he said, his voice quiet.

"But with you, it feels alive."

That night, when the city finally fell silent, she wrote in her journal:

Wish #19: To speak my heart freely and fully, to let my voice rise with all that I am, holding nothing back.

Glitterella sat by the narrow window of her guestroom, her journal open on her lap, her pen poised above the page. She hardly slept all night; she had replayed Caleb's words on the bridge: "Because of you." They had echoed with the bells, with the violin's song, with the snow swirling around them. Her heart knew the truth. She loved him.

But her inner thoughts whispered even louder:

What if he doesn't love you for you? What if it's just the music he wants to do with me? Or his path carries him farther, beyond Prague, beyond me?

She pressed the pen to the page, and the words spilled out as if they had been waiting all along.

Dear Caleb,

When I sing with you, I don't feel small. I don't feel afraid. I feel like my voice belongs in the world, like the music is enough because you hear it.

When you smile at me across the stage, it feels like the lanterns of the Grove all lit at once. When you hold my hand on these cold nights, it feels like I'm home, even though we're across the sea. I am falling in love with you, and it terrifies me more than any stage ever could.

Because what if you don't feel the same? What if this is just a song for you, and for me it's everything?

Still, if I could wish one thing now, it would be this: to find the courage to tell you, not on paper, but face to face.

Yours, always,

Glitterella

Her hand shook as she signed her name. Tears blurred the words until the ink bled slightly, as if the page itself wept with her.

She folded the sheet carefully, tucking it into the back pocket of her journal. For a long moment, she stared at it, her heart pounding.

Give it to him, her courage whispered.

Don't, her heart argued. *What if it ruins everything?*

She snapped the journal shut.

The snap rang small and sharp in the quiet. A faint thread of light ran along the journal's edge, as if asking a question, she wasn't ready to answer.

Later, in rehearsal, Caleb teased her about her serious face, strumming some silly chords until she finally laughed, as he smiled at her with that open, steady warmth she loved.

She thought of the letter in her journal pocket, burning like a secret flame. She wanted to pull it out and hand it to him. She wanted to speak the words aloud. But she didn't.

Instead, she tucked the journal deeper into her bag, where her heart could hide a little longer.

That night, lying awake in her narrow bed, she whispered into the dark:

Wish #20: To be brave enough to let my heart be heard, not just my voice.

The bells of Prague tolled the hour, carrying her wish out into the snowy air.

And the letter stayed where it was, written, folded, and safely hidden for now.

CHAPTER NINETEEN

Thoughts Between Them

The days after the showcase seemed blurred with rehearsals, lessons, and the constant hum of music in the halls. Yet for Glitterella, everything felt muted, as though a veil had slipped over her heart between her and the world.

The letter was still hidden in the back of her journal, burning like a coal she dared not touch. Every time she thought of it. Every time Caleb looked at her with that steady warmth, her throat closed with words she couldn't speak. So, she grew quiet, with a quiet edge, heavy with unsaid things. Caleb noticed.

One evening, on the town, they ducked into a small restaurant for dinner, tucked between narrow cobbled streets. The windows were glowing with amber light, and the smell of roasted garlic and butter drifted out into the cold, enticing them to give it a try.

They shed their coats and found a corner table by a small fireplace inside. Candles flickered between them. She ordered goulash, thick with paprika, served in a bread bowl that steamed in the chilly air. Caleb chose roast chicken with thyme, golden-skinned and fragrant. They shared a plate of dumplings dusted with herbs.

Glitterella found herself stirring her spoon through the goulash more than eating. Caleb leaned on his elbows, watching her with those eyes, catching the candlelight so they seemed to shift between amber and gold. Eyes she could never quite investigate for long, because they always seemed to see too much.

"You've hardly touched your food," he said gently.
"I guess I'm not that hungry after all," she forced a smile. "Just a little tired."
He studied her a moment longer. "You've been saying that a lot."

After dinner, they walked through the square, snow falling in soft spirals. Glitterella hugged her coat tighter, her breath clouding in the frosty air. Caleb walked beside her with his guitar case slung across his back.
Finally, halfway across the Charles Bridge, he stopped.

"Glitterella, you've been way too quiet," he said softly. "It's not like you."
Her heart thudded. The truth pressed against her lips, she couldn't take it anymore, and in her mind, she blurted out...

Because I love you, Caleb. Because I'm terrified you don't love me back. Because I'd rather stay silent than risk losing what we have.

Instead, she shook her head. "I'm fine. Really."
He held her gaze for a long moment. His breath misted in the air, his eyes searching hers as if trying to find what she was hiding. "You don't have to lie to me," he said quietly. "If something's wrong, tell me. We've always carried things together."

Her heart ached. She wanted to fall into his words, to hand him the letter folded in her journal, to let him know the truth she couldn't speak. But the unknown tightened its grip. *If you tell him, you'll lose him.*
"I'm fine," she said again, too quickly.
The shadow passed over his face. He nodded, but it wasn't the easy nod she knew; it was heavy, tinged with doubt.

He lifted his guitar case back onto his shoulder and walked beside her, the silence between them growing wider. This time, their footsteps didn't sync.

Later that night, she sat on her bed with her journal open, staring at the folded letter. She traced its edges with her fingertip, fighting tears. *Wish #21: To find a way to let my love shine instead of hiding it in silence.*

She shut the journal, burying it under her pillow. The bells of Prague tolled again, heavy and mournful, as if echoing the shadow that had slipped between them.

Caleb strummed his guitar softly in his room, wondering what he could have done wrong... then humming a melody quite low, wistful, and feeling alone.

The week after the showcase glittered with all kinds of invitations. Maestro Rinaldi called Caleb aside after rehearsal, his sharp eyes bright. "Caleb, you're playing has improved tremendously. A chamber ensemble is preparing for its Vienna tour. They need a guitarist with your talent and presence. You should audition."

Caleb accepted without any hesitation, his smile quick but guarded when he glanced at Glitterella.

"That sounds... amazing, I will. Thank you."

Word spread fast. Other students began inviting him to late-night jam sessions in the practice rooms, to coffeehouses where improvisations spilled past midnight, to rooftop gatherings where songs rose into the star-thick sky. He said yes to nearly everything.

Glitterella watched. She told herself it was good; he deserved these chances; he deserved to shine. But each time she saw him laughing with a new circle of musicians, each time she passed a practice room and heard his guitar weaving through someone else's voice, the folded letter in her journal burned hotter.

If you had spoken sooner, maybe he would still be by your side?

Her silence grew heavier. She rehearsed alone, her keyboard sounding thin in the echoing halls. She walked the Charles Bridge at night by herself with her journal pressed close, and the river carrying her unsung words away.

Caleb noticed her distance, but he did not press again. He filled the spaces with music instead. He didn't want to upset her or ruin their relationship.

Once, she crossed the atrium as he finished a run with the chamber ensemble. The girl with the silver lanyard stood close, praising his phrasing; another student patted his shoulder and called him "Vienna boy" like a promise. Caleb looked over the heads, searching, and found Glitterella on the balcony. Relief lit his face, then someone tugged his sleeve, and the moment slipped away.

One afternoon, they shared a table in the conservatory café, his hair mussed from rehearsal, his hazel-green eyes shadowed with exhaustion. She sat with her journal closed, hands curled tight around a cooling cup of tea. "You're quiet again," he said, not accusing, but not playful either. She forced a smile.

"I'm fine."

He nodded slowly, then looked away, "You always say you're fine, but it doesn't feel like it." As he was tapping a rhythm pattern on the table as if the wood itself were guitar strings. The silence that lingered between them ached worse than any harsh word.

That night, Glitterella sat outside a practice room where Caleb played with two violinists, laughter spilling between chords. His music was bright, alive.

For a moment, she saw him as if from far away: not just Caleb the boy she loved, but Caleb the musician rising into a world larger than either of them.

And she wondered:

If he goes to Vienna, if he keeps saying yes to every door that opens, will there still be space for me?

She turned away before he noticed her, tears stinging her eyes. Later, in her room, she opened her journal to the folded letter. She unfolded it, read the words again, her heart bared in ink, and almost tore it in half. But she couldn't. Instead, she pressed it back between the pages, as if hiding it deeper might hide her real feelings.

Wish #22: To keep from losing him, no matter what.

She closed the book and curled into herself as the bells tolled over Prague. In the distance, faint but distinct, she could hear Caleb's guitar through the stone walls, brighter than ever, yet somehow farther away.

The distance was growing. And it was her silence that had caused it. She set the journal on the windowsill. Frost feathered the glass in pale ferns. For a long moment, nothing happened, no spark, no shimmer, only her breath and the river's hush. Then, the thinnest line of gold stitched across the page and tugged, so gently she might have imagined it, pointing somewhere beyond the rooftops. Vienna. She pressed her hand flat over the glow until it faded. "Not yet," she whispered to the dark. "Please… not yet."

CHAPTER TWENTY

The Breaking Point

Glitterella stood at the railing, on the Charles Bridge, She had promised herself there would be time to find the courage to finally open her heart. But maybe time had run out.

"Glitterella."

Her name cut through the storm, low and strained. She turned. Caleb was striding toward her, his shoulders rigid with a tension she had never seen in him before. When he stopped in front of her, silence pressed down, heavy as the snow.

"We need to talk," he said. His voice was steady, but his eyes, usually warm and playful, were shadowed now, darkened by hurt.

She swallowed. "Okay."

"You've been pulling away." The words tumbled out sharply. "You barely laugh with me. You barely look at me. You answer when I ask, but it's not real. It's like you're here, but not here. And I don't know why."
He stepped closer, the lamplight catching the snow in his hair.

"I thought we were in this together. I thought,"

His voice faltered, then steadied. "But maybe I was wrong."

Glitterella's heart pounded. The truth burned inside her: Because I love you. Because it terrifies me. Because if you don't love me back, I'll lose everything.
But she still bound her tongue from speaking her true feelings.

"I'm sorry," she whispered. "I just don't know how to,"

"Don't know how to what?" His voice cracked. "Don't know how to trust me? Don't know how to let me carry what you're carrying?

Glitterella, if you don't want me here, if you don't need me,"
He drew a shaky breath, his hands clenching at his sides. "Just say so."

Her lips parted. The words trembled there, fragile as glass. But nothing came.

Caleb waited a heartbeat longer, pain flashing across his face. Then he shook his head and turned, his footsteps crunching away through the snow.

The sound of him leaving split her heart wide. Panic surged. She felt her courage snap loose, wild and desperate.
"Caleb!"

He stopped; shoulders hunched against the storm but didn't turn.

Her voice broke out, raw and shaking: "I love you!"

The words hung in the frozen air, louder than the bells tolling overhead, louder than the river's rush below. He froze. Slowly, he turned back toward her, snow clinging to his lashes, his expression stunned, almost disbelieving.

Glitterella's tears spilled hot against the cold. "I love you," she said again, firmer this time, as if saying it twice might keep it from breaking. "I've been so afraid to lose you, I thought staying quiet would keep you close. But it only pushed you away. I'm sorry. I love you, Caleb."

For a long moment, he didn't move. The storm swirled between them, the lanternlight trembling in the wind.

Then Caleb crossed the space in two strides... He cupped her face in his hands, his touch warm despite the snow.

"You think I don't feel the same?" His voice was hoarse, but his smile was breaking through, fierce and tender. "Glitterella, I've been falling for you since the first day I met you. I've been waiting for you to say it first.

Her breath hitched. "You... have?"

He laughed softly, forehead pressing to hers. "Every song we've played, every note, we've been writing it together. And I don't want to play without you."

On the Charles Bridge, Glitterella stood trembling, her heart raw from the words she had finally let go.
Her words... I love you.
They hung in the air, fragile but glowing.

Caleb's hands framed her face, his touch warm even as snowflakes clung to his hair and lashes. His eyes searched hers, hurt fading, replaced by something fierce and shining.
"You don't know how long I've wanted to hear you say that Glitterella, I love you so much ... it hurts," he whispered.

Tears blurred her vision. "I should have told you sooner. I was afraid... that if I said it, I'd lose you."

His thumb brushed gently across her cheek.

"But Glitterella, love doesn't break when you speak it. It grows."

The river rushed below, bells tolled across Prague, and for the first time, her heart felt free of its silence.

The snow still fell over Prague, soft and relentless, as if the city itself wanted to muffle the world for this one moment. The bells tolled across the rooftops, scattering echoes into the night.

She let out a sob that turned into a laugh, the sound catching in the winter air. Caleb pulled her into his arms, holding her so tightly she felt the strength of his promise in every breath.

For a moment, it was just them, two hearts pressed close, the river rushing below, the city blurred by storm. When they pulled back, his forehead rested against hers, their breath mingling in the cold. The space between them hummed like the pause before a song's crescendo.

"May I?" Caleb asked softly, his voice low.

Glitterella nodded, and his lips found hers, gentle, tentative at first, then deepening with the certainty of love no longer hidden. The kiss was not just passion, but release: every silence, every unsent word, every folded letter finally given its voice.

When they parted, she laughed again, breathless, her cheeks flushed with more than the cold. "What happens now?" Caleb smiled, his arms still around her. "Now? We keep falling in love and singing. Together."

Her heart swelled. "Even if Vienna calls you away?"

His smile softened. "Especially then. Because love isn't about staying in one place. It's about carrying each other wherever we go."

She thought of the Grove, of Aunt Betty June's words: Your song doesn't leave home when you do. It carries home with it. Maybe love was the same. She dropped her journal, and Caleb bent down and picked it up from the snow, brushing it carefully clean.

She pressed the journal to her heart and thanked him, her laughter soft and grateful.

They stood together at the railing, snow drifting down around them. Suddenly, for the first time, Glitterella felt her heart was truly free, her voice, her love, her courage all rising as one.

The morning after their love confession, Prague woke even brighter under a sky of winter blue. Snow shimmered on the rooftops like scattered glass. For Glitterella, everything felt different, lighter, sharper, as if the whole city had been remade overnight.
Love had been spoken. Her silence had been released, and Caleb had finally kissed her.

She carried that memory like warmth in her heart as she walked through the conservatory doors, but in the grand hall, reality waited. Students clustered around the notice board, their voices buzzing. A new sheet of parchment had been pinned up:

Vienna Chamber Tour, Final Selection.

Her breath caught when she saw Caleb's name written in elegant script among the chosen.

Caleb himself stood a few paces away, shoulders squared, though his expression was unreadable. When he turned and saw her, his smile came, soft and hesitant. "You saw it," he said. Glitterella nodded, her heart pounding. "Vienna."
He exhaled, running a hand through his hair.

"It's... everything I've worked for. A chance to play in halls that have held music for centuries. To be part of something bigger."

She forced a smile. "That's incredible."

But inside, her heart tightened. *Bigger than us?*

Finally, she asked,

"When would you leave?"

"Two weeks," he said quietly. "If I say yes."

The words stung. She looked at him sharply.

"If? You haven't decided?"

He shook his head. "I don't want to leave without you."

His voice was low, raw.

"Not now. Not when we've just,"

He broke off, searching her face. "Glitterella, this changes everything."

Her throat ached. She wanted to tell him she would follow him anywhere, across oceans, across stages. But her thoughts stirred in her mind...

That night, she sat at her window with her journal open. The folded letter lay pressed between the earlier pages, no longer unsent, but unnecessary now that her love had been spoken. She flipped to a blank page and wrote:

Wish #23: To love with courage, even when the future pulls me in different directions.

The bells of Prague tolled through the night, solemn and beautiful, as if the city itself was reminding her that every song, even the brightest, must one day change key.

Caleb knocked softly at her door. When she opened it, he stood there,

"May I come in?"

uncertainty shadowing his smile.

"Vienna beckons," he said simply.

"But so does my heart. And it's with you."

Glitterella's pulse quickened. She didn't yet know what answer she could give him. But she knew the future was calling, and love would have to answer.

Glitterella pondered as all the beauty of Prague blurred her mind beneath a haze of questions, regarding Vienna, with Caleb's name printed among the chosen. She thought about the words he'd spoken: "I don't want to leave you behind."

The thought of losing him so soon after finding the courage to tell him she loved him made her heart ache.

She wandered through the conservatory halls, distracted, sitting in class and barely hearing Maestro Rinaldi's instructions. That night, she sat by her window, the river gleaming under the moonlight, her journal open to a new page, which seemed to demand an answer she wasn't ready to give.

Finally, she pulled out her phone with trembling hands and dialed a familiar number.
"Aunt Betty June?"
The warm, steady voice answered almost at once.
"Glitterella! My star across the sea. I miss you terribly... how are you doing, darling?"

Hearing her aunt's voice cracked something open in her. Tears welled, spilling faster than words.

"I don't know what to do." Aunt Betty June let her cry quietly, her patience a comfort even through the distance. When Glitterella finally spoke, her voice trembled. "Caleb's been invited to Vienna. It's... everything he's dreamed of. And part of me wants to go with him. But another part," She broke off, clutching her journal. "Another part feels like if I leave Prague now, I'll lose my own future in music before it's even really begun."

"Hmm," Aunt Betty June said thoughtfully. Glitterella could picture her, hands wrapped around a teacup, eyes kind and wise. "Sounds to me like you've come to your first real crossroads in life and love."

Glitterella grabbed a facial tissue, wiping her tears.

"What if I choose wrong? What if staying means losing him? What if going means losing myself?"

"My girl," Aunt Betty June said gently, "you don't lose love by following your own path. Not if it's true. Love isn't a tether that ties you down. It's a thread that stretches, that carries you both even when the roads bend in different directions."

Glitterella wiped her eyes again.

"But what if it breaks?"

"It won't." Aunt Betty June's voice softened.

"Do you think the Grove stopped holding you just because you crossed an ocean? Home is still with you. Love can be the same. It doesn't vanish when you're apart, it deepens, if it's true and if you tend it."

Her words sank deep.

When the call ended, Glitterella sat still for a long time, the phone turned off, but still in her hand.

Outside, the bells began to toll, their sound carrying across the city like a steady heartbeat. She opened her journal and wrote:

Wish #24: To trust that love can stretch across the oceans, reach through the waves, and still hold when it's real.

She stared at the words until her tears blurred them. Then she pressed her palm to the page, whispering to herself: "I don't have to choose between my voice and my heart. I must be brave enough to trust and carry both." The thought didn't erase the ache. But it gave her a possible beginning.

CHAPTER TWENTY-ONE

The Farewell Looms

A letter arrived on a Thursday afternoon, delivered by a conservatory assistant with cheeks pink from the cold. Caleb unfolded it at the café table where he and Glitterella sat, steam rising between them from untouched cups of tea.

His eyes moved across the page once, then again, slower this time. The muscles in his jaw tightened.

Glitterella's heart sank. "What does it say?"
He set the paper down gently, as if its weight could break the porcelain tabletop. "Vienna. The tour begins sooner than expected. They want me there in ten days."

Ten days?

The words echoed inside her like a bell struck too hard, reverberating until her breath caught. Ten days until the music that had bound them across oceans would carry him farther away, but only a train ride to see him.

They walked the cobbled streets in silence afterward, Caleb carrying the letter about his Vienna trip folded in his coat pocket, his hand brushing it now and then as if to check it was still real. Glitterella, getting a chill, hugged her coat tight, her journal heavy in her bag. She wanted to reach for his hand, to hold onto him as though that could slow time...

Finally, Caleb spoke. "It's everything I dreamed of. And yet," His voice broke. "All I can think about is not leaving you."

Her throat tightened. "You'll do well there," she said, her voice barely above a whisper. "You have to go."

"I don't want to go without you," he said, "What if this takes me away too far and we get too busy for each other?"

She stopped walking, turning toward him. Snowflakes clung to his lashes, some melting before they could settle. She reached up, brushed one away with trembling fingers. "Then we'll find a way."

Caleb's breath shuddered out, a small smile tugging at his lips. "I want to believe that I don't want to lose you or have some dashing handsome Prince whisk you away..."

"Believe it Caleb, you are the only dashing Prince I could feel this love bursting in my heart for," she said, though her own voice shook.

That night, he found her in a quiet practice room, its tall windows glowing pale with moonlight. Caleb shut the door behind him, setting his guitar against the wall.

"We can't let this goodbye be just silence," he said. "Let's write one more song. For us. For Prague. For the thread between us."

Her heart swelled. "We'll make it a song that lasts forever."

They sat side by side at the piano, their shoulders next to each other. They kissed tenderly, and Glitterella turned to her keyboard pressing tentative chords, while Caleb picked up his guitar and caught them, spinning harmonies around her melody. She scribbled the words and then rewrote them many times until they were perfect in her journal, ink smudging as her gentle tears slipped down over the pages.

Time cannot erase us.
We are forever bound.

I'll hear your heartbeat
In every note and sound.
If the river drifts between us,
We'll play through the dark.
No distance can silence
the love within our hearts.
Love carries our name.
No one can betray...
We're written together,
and we'll never fade away.
When the night feels too quiet,
I'll whisper your tune.
And I'll hear it returning
Like the tide to the moon.
So let this be our promise,
wherever we roam,
Love will never leave.
It will always lead us home.

Caleb read the lines again over her shoulder, his hand resting lightly on her back.

"That's it. That's our heart's promise."
They played until dawn, their voices weaving into something tender and fierce. By morning, the song was beautiful and complete.

Two nights later, under the glow of the Winter Festival lanterns in Old Town Square, they performed it. Crowds pressed close, breath rising in clouds, faces turned toward the stage. The melody carried upward into the frosted air, across the spires, over the river.

When they finished, the applause was warm and endearing. As the crowd dispersed, Caleb leaned close, his voice low so only she could hear. "Do you see it now?

They weren't just moved to applause by our song. They felt the love we share."

Glitterella swallowed, her heart trembling. "You mean,"

"The gift from above," he said gently. "The light you've been hiding. I see it every time you sing, and tonight… so did they when we sang together, we are meant to be."

She blinked back sudden tears, the relief of being known, fully known, settling like warmth in her spirit.

But secondary, the true moment was in the way Caleb looked at her, his eyes steady, filled with the knowledge and love of what they had built together. A song that would carry them through the distance.

That night, in her journal, Glitterella wrote:

Wish #25: To trust the light within me, even when I cannot see the path ahead.

Wish #26: That love will keep singing, even when voices are far apart.

Ten days remained. But now they carried a song that could not be silenced; it would live forever.

The station brimmed with winter light and noise. Steam hissed from the engines, carrying the smell of coal and metal into the sharp air. Announcements echoed through vaulted ceilings, mingling with the clatter of boots, the murmur of families pressed into last embraces.

Glitterella clutched her journal against her heart, her breath clouding in the chill. The folded letter, once her secret was still tucked within its pages, though now her love was spoken. Yet it weighed heavily, as if reminding her of every word she'd almost left unsaid.

Caleb stood beside her, guitar slung over his shoulder, his dark coat buttoned against the cold. He looked both radiant and restless, his name already called by the future.

The train to Vienna hissed, a great beast impatient to be gone. She no longer feared her gift. The shimmer was never meant to be hidden; it was a doorway, a glow of light stretching from above into every heart it touched. And now she was ready to carry it wherever her song was called.

Glitterella's throat tightened. Her voice broke as she whispered, "I hate that you're leaving. Every part of me wants to hold on. But I know this is your dream… and I don't want to stand in the way of your future."

Caleb's eyes locked with hers, steady yet full of ache. He reached for her hand, their fingers knotting together as though neither could bear to let go.

He said, "You've already given me everything, your voice, your courage, your love. I don't know how to walk away from that."

Her tears spilled over, trembling on her lashes. "Then don't," she pleaded, her lip quivering.

He drew a shuddering breath, his voice raw. "Then come with me."

The words silenced the noise around them. For a heartbeat, the world shrank to just the two of them, their hands clutched tight in the press of the crowd.
"Come on… come with me, Glitterella.

To whatever comes after. We can write together, sing together, live this dream side by side. Say yes, and we won't have to say goodbye."

Her heart surged. Every part of her wanted to throw herself into his arms, to run onto that train and never let go. She imagined the stages, the lights, the music, Caleb always there beside her.

But beneath the swell of longing was the steady voice within: If you go now, will you lose your own path? Will you become only his echo instead of your own song?

Her tears spilled hot on her cheeks. "Caleb... I want to. More than anything. But what if, what if my journey is here? What if I lose myself by leaving?"

His face broke, torn between love and desperation. "You won't lose yourself. You'll find more. And if you stumble, I'll remind you who you are. Just like you've done for me."

The whistle blew sharply and finally. Conductors called. Passengers surged forward.

Caleb cupped her face in both hands, pressing his forehead to hers. "Say yes," he whispered fiercely. "Say yes, and we'll never let go."

Glitterella trembled, her journal pressed hard against her heart. She wanted to say yes. She wanted to be braver than she had ever been. Her voice cracked as she said slowly, "I don't know if I can."

Caleb's eyes searched hers, raw with longing and hurt. He kissed her, quick and fierce, the kiss of someone who didn't know if it was hello or goodbye.

Then the final call came. He pulled back, his hand slipping from hers, and stepped onto the train.

She stood frozen on the platform, her heart breaking as the train lurched forward. Caleb leaned out the window, his voice carried above the roar:

"Glitterella! Whether you come or stay, I'll love you! Always and forever!"

She clutched her journal, sobbing as the train carried him away until he was gone in the distance.
The bells of Prague tolled overhead, mournful and magnificent, as if the whole city grieved with her.

Prague was quieter without him.
The bells still tolled each hour, their voices spilling over rooftops and spires, but to Glitterella they sounded muted, hollow, as though someone had stolen their echo.

The streets were still alive with winter markets, the smell of roasted chestnuts curling through the air, but each laugh she heard only reminded her of the one that no longer walked beside her.

She wandered the Charles Bridge at night, journal pressed against her heart, listening to the river's restless rush. The statues loomed dark in the snow, silent witnesses to her grief. Here was where she had confessed her love to Caleb.

Every corner of the city whispered of him. The café where they had shared dumplings and laughter. The conservatory practice rooms where their melodies had intertwined. The square where their last song had risen into lanternlight. Each place felt empty now, like a stage abandoned after the curtains closed.

For days, she drifted through rehearsals like a ghost, her music thin, her smile a mask. Maestro Rinaldi frowned once, laying a hand on her shoulder. "Your voice is present, but your heart is not. Where has it gone?"
Her throat burned, but she said nothing.

At night, she opened her journal, staring at the folded letter she no longer needed but could not throw away. She wrote new wishes in trembling hands:
Wish #27: To be brave enough to let love guide me.
Wish #28: To follow my heart, even across oceans.

The more she wrote, the clearer it became: the silence she carried now was worse than any fear she had known before. She had thought staying behind would protect her. Instead, it had broken her.

On the fifth night after his departure, she stood on the bridge once more. She whispered into the storm: "I can't lose him. Not when I've just found him. Not when my heart already sings with his."

And in that moment, she knew.
Her place was not behind, staring at his absence. Her place was with him.

The next morning, she packed only what mattered most: her journal, her keyboard, and Aunt Betty June's old scarf that still smelled faintly of lavender. With trembling hands, she bought her ticket, the ink smudging beneath her thumb as if her own heartbeat had marked it. Her pulse thudded against her ribs, not with fear but with inevitability, like she was racing toward a destiny she could no longer hold back.

The train roared forward through snow-washed fields and forgotten towns. Frost painted the windows with ghostly patterns, but she barely noticed. Each station blurred into the next. Somewhere between waking and dreaming, she dialed his number. Her voice quivered but carried through the line:

"Hold on, Caleb. I'm coming. Meet me at the station. I'm on the last train out."

Vienna rose around her at last, a cathedral of glass and iron, its vaulted roof spilling daylight across the polished stone below. The air was alive with echoes: shoes tapping, voices rising, trains sighing in and out like the lungs of the city itself. She stepped down onto the platform, breath shallow, eyes frantic.

And then, she saw him.

Caleb stood alone beneath the arrivals board, his coat collar pulled high against the cold. No guitar slung over his shoulder, no shield of music to hide behind, just him. His posture sagged with exhaustion, but the moment his gaze found hers, all weariness shattered like glass.

"Glitterella?" His voice cracked, raw, as though he'd spoken her name a thousand times in silence and had almost stopped believing it would ever leave his lips again.

Her bag thudded to the ground. She ran.

He caught her halfway, arms wrapping around her so fiercely she felt her feet lift from the earth. He clung to her as if letting go would undo the world itself.

"I couldn't stay," she sobbed into his shoulder, her tears soaking the wool of his coat. "I thought I had to choose between my voice and you, but my heart already chose. It's you. Always you."

His lips pressed against her temple, her cheek, the line of her jaw. Each kiss was a broken prayer made whole again. His words trembled out, fractured by relief:

"You came. You really came."

She pulled back just far enough to see him, her laughter colliding with tears. "I'd follow you anywhere,

Caleb, Vienna, Paris, even the ends of the earth. Just promise me… don't leave me again."

"Never." His forehead leaned against hers, his hands steady at her waist. His voice carried a vow that no melody could rival.

"Wherever I go from now on, it's only with you."

And then he kissed her again… long, certain, fierce with the knowing that after so many false endings, this was finally home.

That night, Vienna unfolded for them like a dream reborn. They walked hand in hand beneath lanterns glowing softly against cobblestones. Music spilled from open doorways where strangers laughed, fiddles sang, and the heartbeat of the city joined their own. Snow sifted down, quieting every edge, making the world tender and new.

Later, in the hush of their room, Glitterella opened her journal. On its final page, she wrote:

Wish #29: That love, and music, will carry us forward. Together, forever.

The words settled onto the page, and then, light. Many faint sparks shimmered across the ink, golden and soft, stardust breathing between the lines. Her breath caught. It had been years since she'd seen them, not since the Wishing Woods.

Back then, they had frightened her, a burden too heavy to name. But now, with Caleb's hand entwined in hers, she understood they weren't just magic. They were true. They were her vow to sing with honesty, to heal and not wound, to let her gift be a light instead of a shadow.

Caleb's fingers tightened around hers. And then, something extraordinary. The sparks leapt from the page, flowing across her skin and into his hand as well. He startled but didn't let go of her hand. Instead, the light wove between them, glowing over their joined hands like a ribbon of fire.

Her breath trembled.

"Caleb… It's never done this before."

Wonder broke across his face.

"Then maybe it was never meant to be yours alone."

She wanted to believe that, but as the sparks shimmered, she felt something more: not just a blessing, but a condition. The glow lingered, pulsing with their heartbeat, yet beneath it lay a whisper, fragile, and waiting. It was as though the gift had bound them, but not fully. Not yet.

Caleb touched her chin, tilting her face toward his, the golden shimmer mirrored in his eyes. A tremor of breath escaped him before he began to hum, soft, unguarded, a melody as fragile as hope. She had never heard it before, yet she knew it instantly, as though the sparks themselves had been waiting for this moment.

The light pulsed between their joined hands, and words seemed to rise with the music.

Caleb's voice broke the silence, low and certain:

"Heart to heart, forever true…"

The words sank into her like they had always been hers. Breathless, she answered, her voice threading into his:

"Our music lives in me and you."

The refrain shimmered in the air, golden sparks curling brighter around them, their voices entwined. Caleb's eyes widened with wonder, then softened with something deeper. He leaned in, and their lips met as the last notes faded, a kiss long and tender.

The sparks glowed once more, then softened to a quiet shimmer before fading, as if settling into silence. Glitterella held to him, her heart steady, the magic still warm on her skin. She didn't need to understand it yet. It was enough to know the promise had begun.

Slowly, she drew her journal from her bag. The leather still held the faint warmth of the sparks.

"Let's write it," she whispered.

Glitterella took out her pen, and together they wrote the lyrics, line by line, that had just been born between them:

Verse 1

I searched the silence, found only the night,
Then your voice rose, and the world turned to light.
Two wandering souls, one harmony made,
A promise of love that will never fade.

Refrain

Heart to heart, our song will stay,
Guiding us home, come what may.
Every note, forever true,
Our music lives in me and you.

Verse 2

Through shadows and distance, I carried the flame,
Every road whispered the sound of your name.
Now hand in hand, the journey is clear,
The song of forever begins with you here.

Refrain

Heart to heart, our song will stay,
Guiding us home, come what may.

Every note, forever true,
Our music lives in me and you.

As the last line flowed across the page, the margin shimmered faintly, golden sparks breathing between the words before fading into the paper. Their song was sealed, alive in ink, in memory, and in love.

Glitterella pressed her fingers to the journal, then to Caleb's hand. He bent close, his forehead resting against hers. "It's ours now," he whispered.

She smiled through her tears. "Forever."

And then he kissed her again, a final kiss as sure as the promise itself, waiting to be sealed.

A vow yet to be spoken...

Between the Grove and the Castle

PART TWO
The Castle of Light

Chapter Twenty-Two
The Showcase in Prague

Vienna seemed to breathe music. Even in winter, when snow dusted the rooftops and the air smelled faintly of smoke and pine, the streets thrummed with violinists under archways and singers in echoing courtyards. For Glitterella, it felt as if the city itself carried a song, and she and Caleb were now part of its melody.

The rehearsal hall was a cathedral of sound. Strings hummed low, warming up in velvet tones. A clarinet traced darting scales, while a cello answered with a mournful sigh. Caleb sat among them, his guitar resting across his knee, the polished wood glowing under the high windows.

It wasn't just any guitar. The instrument was a restored Stauffer, Viennese-made nearly two centuries earlier, its scroll-shaped headstock and delicate rosette unlike anything she had ever seen. Its tone was warm, articulate, and filled with the city's history. When Caleb first lifted it from its velvet-lined case, Glitterella had felt a shiver, as if the guitar carried not only sound but memory.

Now, as he tuned with careful fingers, she watched from a chair at the side of the hall, her journal pressed tight against her lap. He looked different here, in this circle of seasoned musicians, focused, steady, as though the centuries-old guitar had granted him a place in Vienna's lineage. Yet she noticed the slight rise of his shoulders before the first downbeat, the way his breath deepened to steady himself.

Then he played...

The first notes were soft, almost hesitant, but when the ensemble swelled around him, Stauffer's voice cut clear and sure, threading through violins and winds until it seemed to anchor the whole piece. Glitterella's chest tightened with pride, but also with something sharper. She had felt the golden sparks once, the shimmer that tied her music to something greater, but they had not returned since that night. Watching Caleb command an instrument steeped in Vienna's past, she wondered if perhaps the magic had chosen him now, and her part in it was already done.

The piece ended, applause rising from the musicians themselves. Caleb smiled modestly, but when his gaze swept to the side of the hall, it softened in a way meant only for her.

After rehearsal, he found her waiting at the door. He leaned close, brushing a kiss across her temple.

"Every note I play feels stronger because you're here," he whispered. His voice was steady with gratitude. "Thank you for standing with me, always."

She slipped her hand into his and whispered, "And I always will."

That evening, the ensemble would perform at a private concert in one of Vienna's grand halls, a gathering for patrons and nobles. Glitterella had no idea what waited there, or whose eyes would follow her from across the room. She only knew the sparks had been more silent since the night of their vow but not gone.

Vienna welcomed her with a stage of her own. It wasn't the grand hall where Caleb played with his ensemble, but an intimate salon, walls lined with books and gilded mirrors, a piano tucked beneath tall windows. Patrons sat in velvet chairs; their voices hushed in anticipation. The air smelled faintly of wax and wine, and Glitterella's pulse quickened as she stepped forward.

Caleb stood at the side; the Stauffer guitar cradled in his hands. He gave her a nod, steady and sure, the kind that said: I'm with you.

Her journal rested on the music stand. She opened it, breath shallow, and let the first words guide her voice.

The song rose, fragile at first, then fuller, the kind of song that seemed to come not from her whole being.

The notes curled into the rafters, warm against the gold and velvet of the salon. The patrons leaned forward. A woman pressed her hand to her lips, eyes glistening. A man at the back blinked rapidly, his chest rising in a sharp breath, as though he'd stumbled upon a truth he hadn't meant to feel.

Glitterella felt it too, the shimmer beneath her skin, faint but real, as though the golden sparks were listening. She did not see them, but their memory pulsed in her heart, urging her to give everything to this song.

Caleb's guitar threaded beneath her, each chord a bridge, each note a promise. She glanced at him once, and his eyes lifted to hers with quiet certainty. Together, they carried the melody until it filled the room like a prayer answered.

When the final note dissolved into silence, it seemed the entire salon held its breath. Then, at last, applause erupted, rising like a tide. Glitterella bowed, heat rushing to her cheeks, while Caleb gave the guitar a final resonant flourish.

For a moment, she could hardly believe it; Vienna had listened. And Vienna had understood.

Caleb draped his coat over her shoulders as they walked, their breaths making small clouds in the frozen air.

"You were luminous," he said softly. "Not just your voice. You."

She tucked herself closer beneath his arm. And her heart filled with joy. The city felt unreal, like a dream of spires and lanterns, but Caleb's warmth was steady, grounding her as they reached the great doors of the ballroom.

Inside, the after-party glittered like another world.

Chandeliers blazed above mirrored walls, scattering light into a thousand fragments. Marble floors reflected the swirl of silk gowns, the sharp lines of tailored coats, the glint of jewels at throats and wrists. A pianist played in the corner, coaxing a gentle waltz that threaded beneath the hum of conversation.

Critics and celebrities drifted between clusters of patrons, their laughter bright and polished. The air carried the scent of champagne and roses. Everywhere she turned, eyes lingered on her, some curious, some approving, others whispering words she could not quite catch.

Glitterella stood with Caleb near the edge of the room, a glass of champagne cool in her hand.

Caleb leaned close, brushing his fingers over hers where they met on the glass stem.

"You were radiant tonight," he murmured again, his voice meant only for her. "Vienna won't forget."

Her heart swelled. In the whirl of light and music, he was her anchor, the steady chord beneath the melody.

But then she saw him.

A tall man stood apart from the revelry, near the mirrored wall. Silver threaded through his darkly styled hair, and his coat was cut in an older, sophisticated style, more severe than the glittering fashion around him. He held no glass, joined no laughter. His stillness made the rest of the room seem too bright, too hurried.

Glitterella's pulse stumbled. Something about him, his bearing, his gaze, felt hauntingly familiar, though she could not name why.

Caleb followed her eyes, his expression tightening. Before he could speak, the man crossed the floor. Each step was deliberate, unhurried, as though the crowd parted unconsciously to let him pass.

When he reached her, he bowed his head slightly, his voice low enough that only she could hear.

"You carry her voice."

Glitterella blinked, the champagne trembling in her hand. "Excuse me? I… don't understand."

"Your mother's voice," he said. His eyes at first shocked and then softened, though sorrow shadowed their depths. "And her light. I knew it the moment you sang."

Her breath faltered. "You knew my mother?"

He nodded, slow and grave. "I did. I am Antonín Celestýn, your uncle."

The name struck her like a chord never played yet always waiting. Caleb's hand closed firmly around hers, steady, protective, as if sensing the ground beneath her had shifted.

Antonín slipped a card into her free hand. The paper was thick, the ink precise. His voice dropped to a murmur that threaded beneath the din of the ballroom.

"There are truths you have not been told. The castle has waited long enough."

And then, as swiftly as he had come, he stepped back into the glitter of the crowd.

But the card remained in her palm, heavy as stone. On it, a single word blazed darker than ink: Celestýn.

CHAPTER TWENTY-THREE

Whispers in the City

The champagne glass still trembled in her hand. Glitterella lowered it to the nearest table, afraid it might slip and shatter. The card remained pressed between her fingers, its edges sharp, the single name heavy as if it had been waiting for her all along.

"Glitterella." Caleb's voice was low, taut. He took her hand and guided her gently toward a quieter alcove, away from the hum of conversation and glittering gowns. His hand didn't leave hers, his touch firm as though he feared she might vanish if he let go.

She looked at Caleb in shock, "Did you hear him? He said… he said he was my uncle."

Caleb's brow furrowed. "How could that be?"

"Antonín Celestýn." She held up the card to Caleb. The engraved ink gleamed black under the chandelier's glow. "He said he knew my mother."

Caleb's eyebrows raised, "Do you believe him?"

The question stung, though; somehow, she understood. Everything about the man had been sudden, improbable. And yet, his eyes, the way he said her mother's light, something inside her had stirred, deep and certain.

"I don't know what to believe," she whispered. "But when he looked at me, it was like… like he was seeing something I didn't even know I carried."

Caleb's hand moved to cover hers, closing gently over the card. "Ella, people will say anything when they see a gift like yours. Fame, talent, they attract shadows as much as light."

His words were careful, protective, but underneath them she heard his worry: that she could be hurt, deceived, pulled away.

"He had mentioned a castle she said softly."

That made Caleb pause. His eyes flickered with something unreadable, curiosity, perhaps, or suspicion. "A castle?"

Glitterella nodded, the memory of Antonín's voice still humming through her. The castle has waited long enough.

For a moment, silence hung between them. The party's laughter echoed faintly, distant, like another world.

Finally, Caleb exhaled, rubbing his thumb against her knuckles. "If this is true and he is really your uncle, then there are truths about your family you deserve to know. But not alone. Wherever this leads, we face it together, OK?"

Caleb's steadiness was the one thing she could trust when everything else felt uncertain. She leaned into him, her head brushing his shoulder.

"Together, of course," she whispered.

The following days in Vienna unfolded in slow, golden layers.

In the mornings, they lingered at Café Central, where marble pillars rose to painted ceilings and trays of pastries gleamed under glass. Caleb teased her for ordering too many sweet rolls, and she laughed when he tried to pronounce Apfelstrudel in his halting German.

The café buzzed with poets and philosophers at nearby tables, but in their corner, the world felt smaller, safer.

In the afternoons, they wandered the Belvedere Palace gardens, where statues of marble figures stood cloaked in snow. The air was sharp, the fountains frozen, but Caleb warmed her hands between his as they paused before Klimt's The Kiss, displayed in the palace gallery. Glitterella lingered before the painting, struck by the golden shimmer in the brushstrokes. Something in it felt achingly familiar, like the memory of sparks.

At twilight, they strolled along the Ringstrasse, where gas lamps glowed against the snow and carriages rolled past Vienna's grand façades. Caleb hummed quietly as they walked, fragments of melodies he'd been working through. Each note slipped into her heart as though written for her alone.

At night, they sat side by side in the Musikverein's Golden Hall, bathed in the glory of strings and choirs. The music rose into the ornate chamber, gilded walls gleaming in the candlelight. Glitterella's breath caught as the choir swelled, each voice carrying more than sound, something luminous, almost sacred. She thought of Antonín's words again: your mother's light.

She carried the card tucked in her journal, its weight like a secret heartbeat. Sometimes, when Caleb wasn't looking, she slipped it out and stared at the engraved ink. Celestýn. The name seemed to glow against the page, daring her to claim it.

One evening, as snowflakes whirled against the stained-glass windows of St. Stephen's Cathedral, Caleb caught her expression.

"You're thinking about him again," he said softly.

She startled. "How did you know?"

He smiled faintly, though worry lingered in his eyes. "Because I know you. Your silence is louder than most people's words."

She wanted to tell him everything she was feeling, the strange certainty in Antonín's gaze, the echo in her bones when he spoke her mother's name, but the words tangled. Instead, she tucked the card away and whispered, "I'm just… trying to understand what it all means."

Caleb squeezed her hand. "Whatever it is, Ella, you don't have to face it alone. You know we can go whenever you feel ready."

His words soothed her, but they couldn't quiet the whisper that grew stronger with each passing day:

The castle has waited long enough.

The card burned like a hidden flame inside her journal. For days, she had tried to ignore it, to convince herself that Vienna's beauty and Caleb's steady presence were enough. But the name would not let her go. Celestýn. It whispered in every cathedral echo, every golden note, every silent pause between heartbeats.

At last, one morning, she slipped from their apartment while Caleb tuned the Stauffer by the fire. She told herself she was only walking, only curious, but the card was now in her coat pocket.

At Café Central, she leaned across the counter and asked the server if he had ever heard the name Antonín Celestýn. He frowned, shook his head, and muttered something about "old blood, older than the empire."

At a bookstall along the Ringstrasse, the vendor paused mid-count of coins, eyes narrowing. "Celestýn?

There was once a house by that name. A castle near the forests. People say it's still standing. But some names… best left in the past." He snapped his ledger closed and refused to say more.

And at the market near the Naschmarkt, an elderly woman selling candles crossed herself when Glitterella asked. "Celestýn," she whispered. "A noble family once, yes. Everywhere she asked, the reaction was the same: recognition, quickly shuttered. A flicker of something unspoken. And always, the word castle.

By evening, the weight of it was too much to hold. Caleb had been invited to rehearse with a small ensemble, so she was alone in their room.

With trembling hands, she reached for the telephone to make a call.

"Aunt Betty June?"

A pause. Then her guardian's voice, warm but wary. "Ella? Is everything all right?"

Glitterella swallowed. "I… I need your advice…I met someone here in Vienna after I performed. He gave me his card and said he knew my mother. He said his name is Antonín Celestýn."

The silence on the line was sharper than any word.

When Aunt Betty June finally spoke, her voice trembled. "So, he found you."

Glitterella's pulse stuttered. "Then it's true? He's, my uncle?"

"Yes," Aunt Betty June whispered. "Your mother was born Celestýn. Antonín is her brother. And the castle… it belongs to your family. To you."

Glitterella pressed a hand to her chest. "Why didn't you ever tell me?"

The answer came slowly, heavy with grief. "Because I am not your aunt, Ella. Not by blood. Your mother asked me to care for you when she was gone. I promised her I would keep you safe. That I would protect you from the weight of the legacy until you were strong enough to face it."

Glitterella's throat tightened. The woman who had tucked her in at night, who had baked angel food cakes and kissed her forehead when the world felt too sharp, was not bound by duty of family, but by love alone.

"You mean… you're not my mother's sister?"

"No," Aunt Betty June said, voice breaking. "But I loved her. And I have loved you like you were my own, all your life. That will never change."

Tears blurred Glitterella's eyes, but not from anger. Gratitude welled instead, fierce and aching. "You gave me a home," she whispered. "You gave me love. That's more than blood ever could."

On the other end of the line, Aunt Betty June wept softly. "Your mother would be proud of the woman you've become."

Glitterella clutched the phone, her heart full. She had lost so much, but she had not been abandoned. She had been chosen.

And in the silence between her astonishment and Aunt Betty June's quiet tears, Glitterella understood: Vienna had given her more than music. It had handed her a door and perhaps a new life.

CHAPTER TWENTY-FOUR

Aunt Betty June's Identity

Snow fell in hushed spirals past the tall windows, blurring Vienna into a watercolor of light and shadow. The Stauffer rested against its stand, by the fireplace, its polished wood still holding echoes of Caleb's playing. He leaned forward in his chair, studying her with quiet patience.

"How are you doing? It seems you have been somewhere else all evening," he said softly. "Even when you smile, your eyes are far away. What is it, Ella?"

Glitterella closed her journal, her fingers clinging to the cover as if it might anchor her. She had rehearsed the words again since the phone call, but now they trembled at the edge of her lips. At last, she drew a breath.

"I spoke to Aunt Betty June."

Caleb stilled. "About the man who claimed to be your uncle at the party?"

A flicker crossed Caleb's eyes, concern, suspicion, the familiar protectiveness that always rose when she was unsettled. He said nothing, waiting for her to continue.

"She told me the truth," Glitterella whispered. The words tasted fragile and strange. "As it turns out, she's not really my aunt, not by blood. She was my mother's best friend. It seems my mother asked her to care for me when she was gone, to keep me safe from… all of this." She opened her hand, revealing the card. Celestýn.

Caleb leaned forward, his hands covering hers. "And she confirmed that he is really your uncle?"

Tears blurred her eyes. "Yes. The castle is real. The family is real. And now… It's mine to face."

For a long moment, the only sound was the fire crackling low, the snow brushing against the windows. Caleb searched her face as if memorizing it, the fear, the wonder, the weight of truth settling into her bones.

Finally, he spoke. "Then we should go."

The certainty in his voice startled her.

"You mean now?"

"I mean, you're not facing this alone." His tone was steady, but there was fire beneath it. "If there are truths to uncover, if there's a legacy tied to you, then we'll uncover it together. Whatever waits in that castle, music, secrets, shadows, I'll be there with you."

Her heart swelled with relief and fear entwined. She reached across the table, her fingers slipping into his. "What if it changes everything? What if it changes me?"

Caleb's smile was faint but unwavering. He lifted her hand to his lips, pressing a kiss against her knuckles. "Then I'll love the woman you become just as fiercely as the one sitting here now."

Her breath shivered. The firelight gilded his hair, softened his eyes. In that moment, she knew, he was her anchor, no matter what storms the castle held.

She rose, stepping into his arms. He held her close, her head resting against the steady beat of his heart. For a time, the world outside vanished. There was only the warmth of him, the safety of his embrace, and the quiet vow that passed between them without words.

When she lifted her head, her voice was steady. "Then it's time. We'll go to the castle."

Caleb brushed his thumb along her cheek. "Yes. It's time."

They stood together at the window, watching the snow drift over Vienna's rooftops. The city glowed golden and distant beneath the storm, beautiful and fleeting. Behind it, somewhere beyond the forests, a castle waited in silence.

And soon, they would walk through its gates, together.

That morning in Vienna dawned pale and silver, snow falling in soft veils over the rooftops. The city stirred slowly, shopkeepers brushing frost from their windows, trams rattling faintly in the distance. Glitterella stood at the window of their small apartment, her journal pressed to her chest.

Vienna had welcomed her with music. Vienna had shown her love. And Vienna had given her a name she had never known belonged to her: Celestýn.

"Ready?" Caleb asked gently behind her. His Stauffer guitar in its case gleamed dark in his hand against his long, warm coat. He was leaving with her, not only the city, but the offer to stay, to rise further in its gilded music halls. That knowledge warmed her even as it ached.

"I'm ready," she said.

They spent the morning bidding quiet farewells.

At the Musikverein, Caleb's ensemble clasped his hands and clapped his back. "Vienna will miss you," one violinist said. "But perhaps we will see you again, when the time is right." Caleb smiled, but his gaze drifted to Glitterella as if to say: My music is wherever she is.

At Café Central, the server slipped them extra pastries wrapped in paper, murmuring blessings in German. Glitterella laughed through tears when Caleb mispronounced Sachertorte one last time, and the sound lingered like a farewell note in the air.

At St. Stephen's Cathedral, they lit a candle together, the flame trembling in the drafts of the old stone walls. Glitterella watched the light flicker and thought of her mother, of Aunt Betty June, of the golden sparks that once frightened her and now seemed to beckon her onward.

That evening, they took one final walk through the city. Snow softened every sound, lamps glowed like halos in the mist, and the streets gleamed like polished marble. Glitterella clung to the details, every window aglow with warmth, every note from a distant violin, knowing this chapter of her story was closing.

The train carried them out of Vienna the next morning. They sat side by side, her head resting on Caleb's shoulder as the city receded, the spires shrinking behind drifting snow. The rhythm of the wheels on the tracks was steady, almost like a heartbeat, and for a time they said nothing.

The train pulled out of Vienna with a low groan, wheels catching rhythm as it carved through the frost-lit countryside. Smoke unfurled past the window, dissolving into the pale morning. Glitterella pressed her hand to the glass, watching the city shrink and towers fading to steeples, until only open land stretched before them.

The train gathered speed, crossing rivers that gleamed like ribbons of light. Villages flickered by the conductor's map showed they were leaving Austria behind, crossing the border into South Bohemia, a land of rolling hills and deep pine forests, where the rivers wound like silver threads through the snow. Glitterella leaned closer to the glass. The light here seemed different, older, more watchful, as if it remembered her before she arrived.

The train began to climb, the wheels grinding softly on the grade. Through the window, valleys opened beneath veils of fog. The rhythm of the journey slowed until, at last, the conductor stepped into the aisle and called her stop in a low, accented voice: "Celestýn."

The name struck her like a chord she'd known by heart.

The South Bohemian air was sharp and clean, with a faint scent of pine and snow. The train hissed, exhaled a final breath of steam, and rolled away, leaving her alone beside a weathered stone platform and a wooden sign dusted in frost, Celestýn.

By afternoon, they stepped down at a quiet rural station. They took a taxi from the station to the castle.

The ride took them deeper into the hills. The road narrowed, forests pressing close on either side. Snow whirled across the windshield, blurring the world into white and shadow.

Caleb reached across the seat, taking her hand. "Nervous?"

Glitterella gave a shaky smile. "A little. It feels like… once we see it, nothing will be the same."

"Maybe that's true," he said. "But nothing could change what we are to each other."

The car turned sharply, the trees thinning. And then, at last, they saw it.

The castle rose from the hills like something carved from mist and stone. Towers pierced the gray sky; their spires draped in snow. Walls stretched outward, half-hidden by forest, their windows gleaming faintly with winter light. It looked both timeless and waiting, as though it had held its breath for years, watching for this moment.

Glitterella's breath caught. She clutched Caleb's hand tighter. "It's real."

The driver glanced back, his voice low. "Celestýn Castle."

The name rang through her like a chord finally struck.

And as the taxi wound its way into the courtyard, Glitterella knew she had crossed the threshold of her old life. Ahead lay secrets, inheritance, and a destiny bound in music and light.

CHAPTER TWENTY-FIVE
Arrival at Celestýn Castle

They slowly rolled to a stop before the castle steps.

Waiting at the top of the steps stood attendants, two women in dark uniforms, a man with silver hair and a bow tie, and, at the center, the figure she had already seen once.

Antonín Celestýn.

He looked less severe in the snow light, though no less formidable. His coat was trimmed in sable, his bearing straight as a pillar. Yet when his gaze settled on her, his eyes softened.

"Niece." The word was spoken quietly, but it seemed to fill the courtyard. He extended his hand, gloved in leather. "Welcome home."

Glitterella's fingers trembled as she placed her hand in his. "Thank you," she whispered. Caleb stepped just behind her, watchful, the steady anchor at her side.

Servants whisked their luggage and instruments away, leading them through a great hall lined with tapestries. The air smelled faintly of cedar and candle wax, and their footsteps rang against marble floors.

They were shown to a chamber warmed by a crackling fire. Their room held a tall canopy bed draped in velvet, a carved wardrobe, and a window that looked out over the snowbound forests. A tray of red wine and bread waited on a side table.

"This all feels… unreal," Glitterella murmured, her hand feeling the embroidered coverlet.

Caleb set his guitar gently in the corner. "It feels like a storybook we've stepped into."

That evening, they dined in the great hall. The long table gleamed with silver and crystal, though only three places were set. Antonín presided at the head, his posture regal, his expression measured. Candles burned in a golden candelabra, their flames throwing shadows across the vaulted ceiling.

The light meal passed with little talk, soup rich with herbs, and some sugared fruits. Glitterella tasted everything but scarcely remembered it; her thoughts spun too quickly.

Afterward, they moved into the parlor, where a fire blazed beneath a carved mantel. Caleb poured wine while Antonín settled into a high-backed chair, his gaze never leaving Glitterella.

At last, he spoke. "You have questions. And I have answers."

Glitterella's hands tightened around her glass. "Aunt Betty June just told me the truth," she said, her voice small but steady. "That she isn't really my aunt. That my mother asked her to care for me. That she kept the Celestýn name from me… to protect me."

Antonín's eyes closed briefly, as if the words carried a weight, he had been expecting but still dreaded. When he opened them, grief softened his features.

"Yes. She was not of our blood. She was your mother's dearest friend. When your mother realized her time was short, she begged Betty June to take you away from this place. Away from the burden of our legacy."

His voice dropped, roughened by memory. "Betty June swore she would. And she kept her vow."

The room felt very still.

"Why?" Glitterella whispered. "Why would my mother want to hide me from it?"

Antonín's reply came slowly, heavy with sorrow. "Because the Celestýn gift is not gentle, Ella. It is powerful, yes, light woven with music. But power can wound as much as it can heal. Your mother bore it bravely, but it nearly consumed her."

Glitterella thought of the golden sparks, of how they had once frightened her, how they now shimmered with possibility. "And now it's mine?"

Antonín's gaze flicked to Caleb, then back to her. "Yes. The legacy passes through blood. And now, through to you. But blood alone cannot hold it. It must be bound with truth, with courage, with love. Otherwise, it corrupts. That is why Betty June feared for you. That is why she hid you from it all."

Glitterella set her glass down, her hands trembling. Caleb reached for her hand, steady and warm.

Antonín's voice gentled. "You are not alone now. And perhaps that is the difference."

The fire popped, sending sparks into the chimney. Glitterella felt the weight of his words settle into her bones. Not just inheritance. Not just a castle. A legacy, demanding and inescapable.

The storm eased by morning, leaving the castle hushed beneath a quilt of white. Glitterella woke to silence, broken only by the faint creak of timbers settling and the sigh of wind against the tall windows. Caleb was still asleep, his hand resting near hers on the coverlet; the fire from last night had gone to embers.

She rose quietly, draping a shawl around her shoulders, and crossed to the window. The view stole her breath away. Forests stretched endlessly below, their pines dusted in snow, the river winding dark and silver between them. The world seemed to fall away, leaving only the castle poised above it all, like a crown on the earth itself.

Caleb stirred behind her. "Already up?" His voice was calm with sleep, and his smile softened her nerves.

"I couldn't stay still," she admitted. "It feels like the walls are… listening."

That day, Antonín was called away by business with an advisor from the city. Glitterella and Caleb were left to explore under the quiet supervision of the staff.

The castle was a labyrinth of stone corridors and hidden alcoves. Gilded mirrors reflected candlelight, and portraits of stern-faced Celestýns stared down from the walls. She paused before one painting in particular, a woman with hair like hers, golden threads woven through the dark. The plaque read simply: Elisabetta Celestýn, 1872.

"She looks like you," Caleb murmured, stepping closer.

Glitterella touched the frame lightly, her fingers trembling. "Maybe that's why I feel as though I've been here before."

A maid named Klára, hardly older than Glitterella herself, was dusting the shelves. She glanced over her shoulder before speaking in a low voice. "You must be careful, miss. The Celestýn gift… it brings greatness, but it has broken many hearts.”

Glitterella froze. “What exactly do you mean?”

Klára’s eyes flicked to the door, then back to her. “Your uncle would not want me to say. But the truth is, not every heir has borne it well. Some… were consumed. The light can burn as easily as it can heal.” She lowered her voice further. “Your mother was the brightest of all. And yet, even she could not withstand its full weight.”

Caleb stepped forward, his voice firm but gentle. “Are you saying it’s dangerous?”

Klára bowed her head, her hands clutching the duster. “Dangerous to those who wield it without love. Dangerous to those who let ambition turn it dark. But perhaps…” Her eyes softened as she glanced between them. “Perhaps this time is different. They say the gift shines brighter when two hearts are bound together.”

Before Glitterella could ask more, another servant appeared in the doorway, and Klára slipped quickly back to her work.

Later, in the kitchen, an older cook pressed a roll into Glitterella’s hands with a smile. But her words were hushed, urgent. “Beware the tower room, child. Too many Celestýns have locked themselves away there, chasing visions that were not theirs to see. Promise me you’ll keep to the light.”

Glitterella shivered, clutching the warm bread as though it could anchor her. “Of course, I promise,” she whispered, though she wasn’t certain she understood.

That evening, she and Caleb found themselves alone again in the library. She told him everything, Klára’s warning, the cook's hushed advice, the portrait that seemed to mirror her own face.

Caleb listened in silence, his hand covering hers on the arm of the chair. At last, he spoke. "Your uncle gave us the truth, but I don't think it's all of it. Maybe he thinks he's protecting you. Or maybe…" He doesn't trust us to know everything just yet."

Glitterella turned the roll of bread over in her hands. "And what if they're right? What if the sparks consume me the way they consumed the others?"

Caleb leaned closer, his eyes steady on hers. "Then I'll remind you of who you are. Every day. Every song. You don't carry this legacy alone, Ella. Not anymore."

For a moment, silence stretched, broken only by the crackle of the fire and the faint sigh of snow outside the windows. The golden sparks had not appeared since their arrival, but she could almost feel them now, humming beneath her skin.

Somewhere in this castle lay the truth of her family. Secrets in portraits, warnings in whispers, rooms that held more than stone and shadow.

And Glitterella knew she would have to face them all. Snow pressed hard against the castle windows, the storm rattling through its stone bones. The halls seemed heavier tonight, their silence alive with the weight of things unsaid.

Glitterella had carried the whispers on her own for too long.

When Antonín poured his brandy in the parlor, she stood near the fire, Caleb at her side. The glow from the hearth warmed her, but her voice still trembled as she spoke.

"Why aren't you telling me everything?"

Antonín's hand stilled around the glass. "Everything?"

"The staff speak of heirs who lost themselves. Of a tower room where visions devoured them. Of my mother's gift, consuming her." Glitterella's heart pounded, but she forced the words. "Is it all true?"

Finally, Antonín slowly spoke, his voice raw.

"Your mother was the brightest Celestýn of all. Her light poured into every song, every vow. But she gave too much. She kept nothing for herself. The gift did not kill her; it hollowed her. And when the last of her was gone, the world simply… took her."

Glitterella asked, "And the tower?"

His gaze darkened. "It is a place where the gift lingers dangerously. Too many have sought answers there and lost themselves instead. I forbid you to enter it. Promise me."

But she could not. Not tonight.

Hours later, when the castle lay in shadow, Glitterella sat awake; her mother's name continued to echo in her thoughts.

Caleb stirred beside her, already knowing.

"You want to go see it," he said softly.

She nodded. "Yes… I must."

He rose without hesitation, pulling on his coat. "Then let's go together now."

The stairwell to the tower was cold, spiraling upward into darkness. Each step groaned beneath their feet, as though protesting their climb. Dust and cobwebs thickened the air, and at last they came to a heavy oak door bound in iron.

Glitterella pushed. The hinges moaned, and the room opened before them.

Moonlight spilled across the stone floor. Shelves bowed under the weight of forgotten manuscripts, instruments sagged with age, violins broken, flutes tarnished, and a great harp cracked through its frame. The air carried the dry ache of years.

At the center of a table lay a book, its leather brittle, its pages open.

Glitterella's breath caught as she leaned closer. She knew the handwriting.

Her mother's.

The ink was faded, the words fragmented: "…the light grows stronger…" "…burns if I linger too long…" "…for Ella, I pray she carries it with love, not fear…"

Her fingers trembled over the lines. A sob rose in her with tears forming, "This was hers. She fought it here."

Caleb's arm slid around her shoulders, grounding her. And then she felt it, a strange energy in the room pulling at her. The same hunger that had claimed her ancestors, a whisper that promised: Search deeper. Demand more. Take what power you can.

Her breath came fast. This was the path they had walked, their undoing.

She lifted her head and looked past the broken harp, past the shadows, to the high windows arched against the night. Beyond the frost, stars burned sharp and steady. The heavens stretched wide, waiting.

Her voice shook, but she said what she thought out loud: "No! not like this."

Instead of reaching inward, she turned upward.

Glitterella closed her eyes and let a song rise, soft at first, then steady. Not a summons, not a demand, but a prayer. A plea for light greater than her own.

The air shifted. Warmth brushed her cheek like a touch, and then sparks, golden, tender, weightless, drifted down from the rafters. Not wild, not burning, but gentle as starlight. They gathered around her shoulders, and then over Caleb's hands, where they clasped hers.

He drew in a breath, wonder spilling across his face. "Ella…"

She sang stronger, and his voice joined hers. Their harmony rose, threading upward, filling the room, spilling through stone walls as if the castle itself was reacting.

When the final note faded, the sparks did not vanish. They lingered, pulsing softly, then sank into her mother's journal, sealing the words with light.

Caleb whispered, awed, "I think you broke it."

Tears streamed down her face as she pressed the book to her chest. "No. Heaven did. I only chose differently."

The tower no longer felt haunted. It felt free.

For the first time in generations, the Celestýn curse had cracked, not through power, but through surrender. Through real love.

Caleb kissed her, his voice low. "Then this gift was never meant to be a burden. It was always meant to be a blessing."

Glitterella closed her eyes, resting her head against his shoulder. And for the first time since stepping into the castle, she felt not the fear of legacy, but the strength and heartfelt love to carry it all forward.

CHAPTER TWENTY-SIX
A Changed Heir

Down in the great parlor, a fire burned low and steady, breathing warmth into the hush. Glitterella sat near the hearth, her knees drawn close, her locket resting against her collarbone. The flames licked and whispered, as if remembering the music of her mother's hands. Shadows moved along the carved mantel, alive with the flicker of gold. Caleb's quiet strumming filled the space between heartbeats. Every chord trembled in the air like a question he couldn't quite voice.

Across from them, Antonín leaned back in his chair, his face carved in amber light. His fingers traced the rim of his glass but never lifted it. The silence stretched, taut and waiting. At last, he spoke, the words slow and deliberate, as though each carried the weight of a lifetime.

"The Celestýn gift was never meant to be a weapon," he said. "But pride twists even miracles."

Glitterella straightened, her pulse quickening. "Someone used it to harm?"

He nodded once, his eyes sinking into the fire. "Lucien Celestýn. He learned to wield the light not as song, but as command. He bent hearts. Broke wills. When the music obeys you instead of moving through you, it becomes poison. His power devoured him, and the stain of it has never left these walls."

Caleb set his guitar aside. The sound of its final string faded into the embers. "And my mother?" Glitterella asked, her voice trembling.

Antonín replied, "She tried to heal what he had ruined. She sang to restore the gift, to turn it back to love.

But love can burn just as fiercely. She gave too much of herself, and the light took her strength. Even when she was dying, she asked only one thing, that you be spared until you could choose the legacy freely."

The words broke something loose inside her. Glitterella rose, unable to sit still beneath the crush of memory and mystery. She crossed to the mantel, her hand touching the cold frame of a portrait she had not yet dared to look at closely. A woman's eyes met hers, gentle, luminous, alive with the same flecks of gold that sometimes sparked in her own.

"She looks so young," Glitterella whispered. "So alive. Was she happy here?"

Antonín's gaze softened. "For a time. Until she saw what the gift demanded. She wanted you to have a different life, one where your heart could grow before your light awakened."

The fire popped, scattering embers across the stone. Glitterella turned toward it, the heat warming her face. "Then maybe it's time I stopped running from it."

Caleb rose beside her. "Then let's listen to what it wants to tell you."

Antonín opened his mouth as if to protest, then fell silent. He watched as Glitterella sat down before the hearth, her journal open on her lap. She laid the locket on the page. Her whisper carried like a note through still air. "Show me."

For a long moment, nothing stirred. Then the flames deepened orange to gold, gold to white. The light swelled, rippling like water, and faint music began to hum through the room, not from the guitar, not from any instrument, but from the air itself. The melody shimmered tender, yearning, old as the stones that surrounded them.

A voice rose within it.

"Ella..."

Her eyes filled. "Mother?"

The sound was faint, but it carried through her bones. Love will keep the light true. Fear will twist it. The song is yours now, sing it for truth, not power.

The fire breathed once more, then settled back into its ordinary glow. The echo of her mother's voice lingered like warmth after tears.

Glitterella pressed both hands over the locket. "She's still here," she whispered. "Not haunting but helping."

Antonín's glass slipped from his hand and shattered. He sank to his knees; one hand braced against the hearthstone. "After all this time," he breathed. "Her light never left us."

She turned and knelt beside him, reaching for his hand. "She didn't leave you, Uncle. She just passed it on."

His rough fingers closed around hers, trembling. For a long moment, they stayed that way, two generations bound by loss and forgiveness. The fire painted their faces in amber, softening every line that grief had carved.

Caleb moved closer, his quiet strength grounding them both. He touched Glitterella's cheek gently, catching a tear before it fell. "This gift... It's not a curse, Ella. It's a bridge."

The firelight swayed, a living presence around them. Glitterella could almost feel the castle listening to the stones breathing again, lighter, looser, freer. "Then let this be the beginning," she said softly. "Not of power, but of peace."

Antonín rose slowly, his movements heavy with reverence. "There are still places in this house where darkness lingers," he warned, his gaze turning toward the upper stair that vanished into shadow. "The tower has never stopped haunting us all. Promise me you won't go there tonight."

But she couldn't promise. Not yet. Something in that darkness called her name, not to harm, but to finish the story her mother began.

As the last embers sighed in the grate, Glitterella turned toward the window. Snow drifted past the glass, catching light from the fire. Each flake gleamed for a heartbeat before vanishing into the night. She drew a breath that trembled with hope. "Tomorrow," she whispered, "I'll find what's left and free it."

Caleb's arm came around her shoulders, his warmth steady, his voice low against her hair. "And I'll go with you. Wherever it leads."

They stood together, the fire dwindling to coals. Above them, the tower loomed unseen in darkness, waiting. But in the parlor below, love burned quietly, stronger than fear.

The last spark leapt upward in the chimney, scattering gold against the cold stone, and Glitterella watched it rise.

CHAPTER TWENTY-SEVEN
A Changed Heir

Dawn broke pale, and Glitterella woke slowly, her mother's journal under the edge of her pillow. The embers in the hearth had gone cold, yet she felt warmth lingering in her skin, as if the golden sparks had woven themselves into her very being.

Caleb stirred beside her, "You look… different."

She gave a soft laugh. "Different how?"

"Like the night touched you and left something even more beautiful behind."

When they stepped into the corridor, the staff paused in their duties. The maid who had bowed her head yesterday now looked at her openly, her eyes shining with a mixture of awe and relief. The cook from the kitchen, usually brisk, brought a steaming cup of her favorite tea to Glitterella without a word. She wondered how he knew.

Klára, the young maid who had whispered warnings, leaned close as she passed with a basket of linens. Her voice was hushed, reverent. "The air feels lighter. Whatever was haunting this house… you've not only changed it., but it also feels heavenly."

Glitterella's heartbeat increased, because within, she knew it was true.

Antonín found them later in the great hall. He was not a man easily unsettled, but his gaze lingered on her as though searching for the girl who had arrived the night before and not quite finding her.

"You went to the tower," he said quietly. It was not a question.

Glitterella met his eyes without flinching. "Yes."

For a moment, it seemed he might scold her, demand why she had disobeyed. But instead, his shoulders lowered with something that looked almost like relief.

"And now, his voice low, the castle feels… freer than it has in years." He stepped closer, his expression heavy, "You've done what none of us could do. You lifted your eyes where we buried ours."

Glitterella clutched her mother's journal close. "I didn't break it alone. Caleb was with me. And it wasn't my strength that answered, it was a power from above even greater."

Antonín's gaze flicked to Caleb, then back to her. "Perhaps that was always the lesson. That the gift cannot be carried alone."

The hall fell silent. Sunlight poured through the tall windows, shining on the stone floors, and for the first time, Glitterella did not feel like a guest in Celestýn Castle. She felt like it was now hers.

That morning, Antonín summoned them to the library, its walls lined floor to ceiling with volumes whose spines bore the family crest. A fire glowed in the hearth, and on the table lay a stack of ledgers and a box bound in iron clasps.

He rested a hand on the box before speaking. "For centuries, the Celestýns carried a gift unlike any other, music woven with light. But what began as a blessing had turned into a curse. Power, Ella, has a way of bending even the purest intentions."

Glitterella listened, her hands folded on her mother's journal. Caleb sat close, silent, his steady presence an anchor.

Antonín continued, his voice heavy. "Some Celestýns believed the sparks were meant to set them above others. They used them to sway hearts, to command loyalty, to bend the will of those who listened. They confused the gift for control, and dominion. And it consumed them. That is the curse you've heard whispered." He drew a long breath. "But others, fewer, chose differently. They used the light to heal, to bring peace, to bind rather than break. Your mother was one of them, though even she burned too bright for too long."

He opened the box, revealing brittle letters, broken quills, and fragments of sheet music where faded notes glimmered faintly gold. "This is our history. It's all part of what you will inherit."

Glitterella reached out, her fingers brushing one page where a hymn shimmered faintly, as though the sparks clung even to memory. "And now it will be mine?" she whispered.

Antonín turned to her, "Yes. But perhaps for the first time in our line, you will not carry it alone." His gaze shifted to Caleb, steady and measuring.

Caleb met it without flinching. "I won't let her."

Something softened in Antonín then, a weary acceptance.

The days that followed were quieter, as though the castle itself exhaled after generations of strain. Glitterella and Caleb filled the long halls with music. She sang in the chapel, her voice echoing off the vaulted ceilings, sparks flickering gently in the air like drifting candlelight. Caleb played the Stauffer in the great hall, his chords threading warmth into the cold stone. Together, they composed fragments, songs born of laughter, of whispered prayers, of the harmony that lived between them.

At night, they walked the snowy gardens, their footprints the only marks in the white. In the kitchen, the staff began to hum her melodies under their breath. The castle, once brooding, seemed lighter, as if the stones themselves were remembering joy.

And yet, peace never holds forever.

One evening, as they lingered over supper, a knock echoed through the hall. A messenger stood in the doorway, snow clinging to his coat. His eyes darted nervously toward Glitterella as he bowed.

"A letter, sir," he said, offering it to Antonín.

The seal was foreign, pressed in dark wax. Antonín broke it, his expression tightening as his eyes scanned the page. When at last he looked up, his face was grave.

"Ella," he said quietly. "It seems your inheritance reaches further than this castle. There are those beyond these walls who have not forgotten the Celestýn name."

The fire snapped in the silence that followed.

Glitterella's hand found Caleb's beneath the table, her pulse quickening. The peace they had found was about to be tested.

The letter sat unopened on the library table, its seal pressed in black wax. Glitterella traced its edges with her fingertip, the weight of it pressing heavier than parchment had any right to.

Antonín watched her from his chair by the fire, his hands folded. "It bears your name," he said softly. "But it is not meant for me to open. Nor for now."

She looked up, startled. "Not now?"

He shook his head, his expression unreadable. "The seal carries instructions, clear ones. It is to be opened on your birthday. Until then, it waits."

Her pulse quickened. "My birthday… that's only weeks away."

Antonín's eyes lingered on her, heavy with something she could not name. "Some truths cannot be forced. They arrive at their appointed time."

That night, the staff whispered as she passed. A maid curtsied low, murmuring, "Pray it brings blessing, not burden." Everywhere she turned, her birthday felt less like a celebration and more like a countdown.

Caleb noticed the way she touched her journal more often, the way her smile faltered in unguarded moments. One evening, he caught her hand in the hallway. "Don't let the waiting hollow you out, Ella. The letter's not bigger than you. Whatever it holds, we'll face it together."

His words steadied her, but not enough to quiet the tug of longing and dread she felt.

A week later, a package arrived, wrapped in plain brown paper, carrying a familiar script. Glitterella tore it open with shaking hands. Inside lay a scarf she recognized at once, soft, well-worn, the one Aunt Betty June always draped over her shoulders in winter. And a letter.

She unfolded it carefully.

My Darling Girl,

I hear whispers even here. I know where you are now. I was never meant to keep you forever, only until the time came for you to stand where you are. Please don't think my love for you any less because I hid the truth. I did as your mother asked. I gave you a home, a childhood safe from shadows. If you wish me there, say the word. I will come to you.

There is something else you should know. When your mother placed you in my care, she left enough to provide for us both, not riches, but more than enough to ensure you would never want for food, for warmth, for the little joys that make a childhood sweet. She said it was her way of being with us even after she was gone, of making certain we had a roof above our heads and music in our hearts. Every book I bought you, every lesson, every holiday we spent together, it was her gift as much as mine.

I thought I would carry that secret to my grave. But now the truth has come to meet you, and I can only pray you see my choices for what they were: love, not betrayal. Your mother asked me to guard you from the weight of the Celestýn name until you were ready to choose it yourself. I promised her I would, and I do not regret a single day of keeping that promise.

If you call for me, I will come. I will stand with you in that great house, even if its stones remind me of all I could not protect her from. I love you, Ella. Nothing will ever change that.

Always,
Aunt Betty June

Glitterella read the words aloud to Caleb. Tears blurred her vision by the time she finished. Caleb drew her close, his hand steady at her back.

Across the room, Antonín stood by the mantel, his face turned toward the fire. His silence was not indifference; it was grief.

"She raised you well," he said finally, his voice rough. "Better than I could have. If she comes, it will be her home too. But she will remind me of everything I lost."

Glitterella's heart ached, but she lifted her chin. "Then perhaps it's time we stop living in the past and grieving for what was lost."

That night, as snow swirled outside the tall windows, she stood in the music room with Caleb. He strummed soft chords on the Stauffer, and she sang low, words forming without thought:

A gift can be a burden or be like a flame,
But love turns it into a blessing, not sorrow or shame.

Golden sparks stirred faintly, gilding the air. Caleb's eyes glowed with wonder, his smile tender as he echoed her refrain.

And then, just as the last note faded, she felt something new. A hum beneath her feet, deep and resonant, as though the very stones of the castle carried a secret. She stilled, her hand pressing to the floorboards.

"Did you feel that?" she whispered.

Caleb tilted his head, frowning. "I didn't hear anything."

But she had. Not above, not around, below.

Another place.

The letter was sealed until her birthday. Aunt Betty June's arrival. The hidden chamber waits beneath the castle.

All of it was drawing her deeper. And she knew, her mother's story was not yet finished.

CHAPTER TWENTY-EIGHT
Murmurs Among the Staff

The storm had passed by morning, leaving the castle hushed beneath a glaze of ice. Glitterella walked the corridors alone, following a pull she could not explain.

She stopped before a door she had not yet entered. The maid who tended the hall called it the "east chamber," but as Glitterella pressed the latch and stepped inside, she knew the truth before a word was spoken.

It had been her mother's room.

The air still carried a faint sweetness, lavender and old paper. A writing desk stood near the window, its drawers closed, its surface dusted but untouched. The bed was draped in pale linen, as if waiting for a sleeper who would never return.

Her breath caught as she crossed over to the desk. She opened the top drawer slowly, her fingers trembling. Inside lay another leather-bound journal, its cover worn smooth with use.

She sank into the chair and opened it.

The handwriting was elegant, familiar.

Dearest Ella,

If you are reading this, then my prayers have carried you further than my years could. The gift that burns in our blood is beautiful, but it is not gentle. I carried it with all I had, and in time, it took from me more than my body could bear. The physicians named it exhaustion of the heart. I know it as the cost of giving too much, of pouring light until nothing was left to hold me here.

Glitterella pressed her hand to the page, tears slipping down her cheeks.

The entries went on, day after day, her mother's voice steady even as her health failed.

Do not fear, little one. You are not alone. Betty June will raise you with love, and perhaps that is the greater gift than any legacy. I asked her to keep you from these walls until you were ready, because I could not bear for the shadows of this castle to claim you too soon.

Promise me this, Ella: never give the gift to the point that nothing remains. Carry it with love, not fear. Let it heal. Let it sing truth. But do not let it hollow you as it did me.

If you feel sparks rise when you sing, know they are not chains. They are light. They are memory. They are with me, still with you, always with you.

Glitterella closed the book, caught in a stare. Caleb found her silent in the doorway and crossed to her without a word. He wrapped his arms around her, and she let her tears fall against him.

"She knew," Glitterella whispered. "She knew it would take her away. And still… she chose to keep singing."

Caleb's lips pressed to her hair. "Then maybe the gift isn't about survival. Maybe it's about love worth giving, even at a cost. But you, you've already broken the curse. You don't have to follow her path. You'll carry it differently."

Glitterella lifted her face, looking out the window.

She heard the sound of wheels on gravel outside the castle gates. Glitterella turned to look closer out the window and ran down to open the front door. Just as the taxi door swung open, Aunt Betty June stepped out as her long coat swept against the stones. Snow falling in her hair as she lifted her face up to the towers, eyes shining with something between awe and sorrow.

"Ella," she breathed, her voice carrying warmth through the cold. She gathered Glitterella into her arms, holding her fiercely for a moment that trembled with memory.

They entered the great hall together, the air glowing with candlelight. The long table was set with silver and porcelain, gleaming like moonlight on still water. With four places waiting along its polished length: Antonín at the head, Glitterella at his right, Betty June across from her, and Caleb at her side.

Glitterella's hands rested in her lap, her journal tucked close by her chair. The meal passed in the quiet rhythm of clinking cutlery and the soft crackle of the hearth. Conversation stalled, unspoken words heavier than the pheasant and wine before them.

Finally, Antonín set down his glass. His gaze flicked from Glitterella to Betty June, lingering with a gravity that seemed to bend the air.
"You kept your vow," he said.

Betty June's knife stilled against her plate. Her eyes lifted, steady, though her voice was low. "I did. I promised her, and I kept Ella safe."

"You kept her from me, too." His words weren't accusation so much as confession, threaded with hurt.

Betty June finished a sip of wine.

"You know why. This house would have swallowed her before she could choose. I could not let that happen."

Glitterella looked between them, her pulse quickening. "You mean… all these years, you both knew, and neither of you…"

Antonín's jaw tightened. "I thought I had lost you both." His eyes shifted, not to Glitterella this time, but to Betty June. "Your mother. And you." Betty June's hand trembled as she reached for her wine. "Antonín, it was never about us. It was about her. About Ella. She was like my sister in everything but blood. When she asked me, I had no choice but to say yes."

"Perhaps," Antonín said softly, "but you had a choice about me." The words hung there, a wound laid bare at last. Glitterella's breath caught. She felt Caleb's hand brush hers under the table, steady, reminding her she was not adrift in this storm. Betty June's eyes glistened. "I cared for you. But I loved her more. And when she asked for Ella's safety, that became my life. You… you would have tied me to this place, and I could not. Not then."

For the first time, Antonín looked away, his gaze settling on the flames in the great hearth. "And so, I lost you both."

Silence followed, heavy with everything unsaid.

Then Glitterella spoke, her voice trembling but clear. "But I am here now. Because she trusted you, Aunt Betty June. And because you trusted her. And because, Uncle, you never stopped waiting. Maybe what matters isn't what was lost, but what's here, still."

Her words seemed to soften the edges between them. Antonín exhaled slowly, his voice almost a whisper. "Perhaps you are right. Perhaps her legacy was never meant to be borne by one heart alone."

Betty June bowed her head. "Then let us carry it together now. For her. For Ella."

Glitterella looked at Caleb, who gave her a small, steady smile. The circle was not yet healed, but it was no longer broken.

Later, in the parlor, the firelight softened the shadows. Caleb poured wine into crystal glasses while Antonín and Betty June sat opposite each other, the tension between them gentled into something quieter, still tender, still wounded, but touched by understanding.

Glitterella curled beside Caleb, her mother's journal resting on her lap. For the first time, she felt the threads binding past and present draw close, weaving into something stronger.

CHAPTER TWENTY-NINE
The Chamber of Murals

The morning came with a quiet unlike any she had known in the castle before. No creak of floorboards in the hall, no whisper of servants moving unseen. The air itself seemed to hush, as though the old stones had listened to the night before and now waited to hear what came next.

Glitterella rose and dressed slowly, her mother's journal in her hand, Caleb stirred, watching her with soft eyes from where he sat at the edge of the bed, lacing his boots.

"You feel it too," he murmured.

She nodded. "The castle feels… lighter. As if some shadow lifted when they spoke last night."

Caleb smiled faintly. "Maybe it isn't just them. Maybe it's you. You're the one stitching everyone back together."

"I don't feel what you might call stitched. I feel… more pulled apart. Between what Aunt Betty June wants, what Uncle Antonín waits for, what my mother left behind, and what I want. I don't even know where I belong."

Caleb crossed the room over to her. He touched her cheek, tilting her face toward his. "You belong here." Then his voice gentled, as if he could hear the storm in her heart. "And you belong with me. The rest we'll figure out together."

Her breath shook, but his steadiness anchored her. She leaned into his touch, whispering, "What if I can't be what they want? What if I fail?"

"Then you fail with me at your side. And somehow, we'll stand up again. That's all the promise I can give, but it's one I'll never break."

She pressed her forehead to his chest, letting his warmth quiet the tremor inside her. For a moment, the world narrowed to just his heartbeat, steady and true.

They walked the halls together later that morning, side by side. The staff glanced at Glitterella with new eyes, as if seeing not the girl who had arrived days before but the heir who carried her mother's fire. Whispers followed her, Celestýn… sparks… chosen…

At the foot of the grand staircase, Antonín waited, his coat buttoned, his cane tapping lightly against the marble. Betty June stood near, her scarf draped across her shoulders, her gaze softer than Glitterella had ever seen.

"The castle is awake again," Antonín said simply. His eyes rested on Ella, "It's feeling you here. It knows you."

Glitterella's hand tightened in Caleb's. She felt the truth of it, the faint hum beneath the stones, like a chord waiting to be struck. The castle wasn't just walls and history. It was alive with memory, and now, with expectation.

Aunt Betty June stepped forward, her voice quiet. "Glitterella, this place will ask much of you. More than you should carry alone. But you are not alone. Remember that."

Ella lifted her chin. "I know. I have both of you. And I have my love." She glanced at Caleb, whose smile was content and sure

Antonín studied the young man for a long moment. At last, he inclined his head. "Then perhaps the legacy will not consume you after all."

That night, Glitterella and Caleb slipped into the music room. He played the Stauffer, strumming the notes low and warm. She opened her journal, the sparks flickering faintly across the page, and she felt peaceful.

They began to play, softly at first, then stronger, their voices and chords weaving into something new. And as the music rose, the castle seemed to listen, its silence vibrating with resonance, as if recognizing the harmony not of one voice but of two.

When the last note faded, Caleb's hand found hers across the keys. "Whatever comes, Ella," he said quietly, "we will face it together. Castle, curse, legacy, all of it."

She nodded, her heart steady and calm for the first time in days. The legacy might weigh heavily, but love, their love, gave it wings.

The days slipped by in quiet rhythm. Snow gathered deep against the castle walls, the forest paths silent except for the cry of crows. Yet beneath the stillness, Glitterella felt something stirring, as if the castle itself breathed differently each day she remained.

Her birthday drew closer. Every time she passed the library, her eyes sought the sealed letter waiting on the desk. She had not touched it again, but its presence pulled at her, a weight of expectation she could not escape.

The staff, too, seemed unsettled. She caught them watching her with sidelong glances, whispering when they thought she was out of earshot. Once, in the corridor, two maids fell silent the instant she stepped into view, one crossing herself quickly, the other muttering, "Not yet, not until the day…"

At supper, the steward, a quiet man with silver at his temples, bowed low and said, "All preparations are being made for your birthday, Lady Celestýn." His words lingered with a weight that made her set down her fork and wonder what was in store for her.

Later that night, she wandered the halls alone. Caleb had gone to the music room, his guitar a comfort in restless hours. Her steps echoed in the long gallery, lined with portraits of Celestýns past. At the end of the gallery, she paused before one portrait, a woman with hair dark as midnight, her gaze fierce yet sorrowful. A brass plate beneath bore a name she didn't recognize: Isolde Celestýn.

The air shifted. Glitterella swore she heard a faint sound, like a chord struck on some distant harp, vibrating through stone.

"Ella?"

Caleb's voice broke the silence as he appeared at her side, concern in his eyes. "You've been gone too long."

She gestured toward the portrait. "Do you hear it? Like music in the walls?"

He tilted his head, listening. "No. Just the wind." But his gaze softened at her expression. "Though if you hear it, then maybe it's meant for you."

She leaned into him, grateful for his steadiness. "It's like the castle is trying to tell me something. Like… there's even more hidden here."

Caleb kissed her cheek and put his arm around her. "Then we'll find it together... Soon, there will be no secrets left to gnaw at you."

The next morning, Antonín summoned her to the library. The letter still sat untouched on the table, its black seal unbroken. He studied her long before he spoke.

"The Celestýn gift is not the only inheritance," he said finally. "This castle is full of chambers and histories even I do not know. Your mother… she may have left more than you realize. And the letter will tell you where to look."

Glitterella, with a surprised look, "But not until my birthday."

Antonín nodded gravely. "Not until then."

Aunt Betty June entered quietly, her expression unreadable. She placed a gentle hand on Glitterella's shoulder. "Whatever it reveals, you'll have us. You won't walk into it alone."

But even as she said it, Glitterella felt the truth settle inside her: when the seal finally broke, the choice of what to do next would rest with her alone.

That night, as she lay awake with Caleb beside her, she whispered into the darkness: "What if it changes everything?"

Caleb moved closer to her, "Then we'll change with it, remember what you said about fear, remember?"

The next evening, the fire in the parlor burned low, its glow painting the stone in gold and shadow. Aunt Betty June sat close, her scarf draped loosely about her shoulders, her eyes distant as if listening to ghosts.

Glitterella leaned forward. "Aunt Betty June… when you lived here, before you took me away, did my mother ever say anything about hidden places?"

Betty June's gaze turned towards Antonín, who sat in the tall chair by the fire. "Not directly. But she wrote. She kept scraps of paper, little notes she tucked into books, pressed between music sheets. She used to say the castle had a heart of its own. That if you listened closely, it would reveal its secrets."

Caleb frowned thoughtfully. "Ella heard something last night. Music in the walls."

Aunt Betty June turned sharply to Caleb.

"You heard it too?"

Ella shook her head.

"Only me. But it was real. I felt it."

Antonín stirred, his face shadowed.

"The Celestýn blood awakens what others cannot hear. But the letter will not be opened until her birthday,"

Betty June met Antonín's eyes across the room. "You'd keep her waiting while the castle stirs around her? That's not what her mother wanted."

For a moment, Antonín's jaw tightened. Then he rose abruptly, muttering something about unfinished correspondence, and left the room.

The silence he left behind was so thick in the air, you could cut it with a knife.

Betty June reached for Ella's hand.

"He fears what you'll find. But I believe your mother left more than warnings. She left a path."

Later that night, unable to sleep, Glitterella wandered the east wing with Aunt Betty June and Caleb. The torches flickered, shadows stretching long across the stone.

At the end of a narrow corridor, Betty June stopped before an old cabinet tucked against the wall.

"I remember this," she whispered. Her fingers traced the wood. "Your mother once told me never to touch it. That some doors were meant only for you."

Ella's pulse quickened. She pressed her palm against the cabinet's edge and felt it tremble, a faint vibration like a string plucked. With a soft groan, the wood shifted.

Behind it, a narrow door revealed itself, dark and waiting.

Caleb exhaled. "Well, that answers one question."

Betty June's grip tightened on Ella's shoulder. "Careful. Some secrets are more dangerous than they seem."

But Ella stepped forward, drawn by the hum of unseen chords. The door opened into a spiral stair, its stones cold beneath her hand. From below came the faintest glow, golden, like sparks dancing in the dark.

She looked back at them, her heart racing. "It's calling."

Betty June's face was pale, Caleb's steady. Together, they followed her down into the depths of the castle.

CHAPTER THIRTY
Shadows at the Gate

The spiral stairs wound downward, their stones slick with age. The faint glow grew brighter with each step, not torchlight, not fire, but something softer, golden, alive. The air warmed as they descended, the scent of cedar and wildflowers replacing the cold of the castle above.

At last, the stair opened into a vast chamber. Glitterella froze at the threshold.

The walls were alive with murals, beautiful angels painted in sweeping strokes, their wings spanning from floor to ceiling. Some carried harps, other violins and cellos, their faces radiant, eyes lifted toward a light that seemed to shine not from paint but from the heaven above. As she moved closer, she saw that the pigments shimmered faintly, as though the colors themselves breathed.

"It's all… so beautiful," Caleb whispered, his voice hushed, reverent.

Aunt Betty June pressed a hand to her mouth.

"I never knew this place existed."

Her eyes glistened.

"Your mother must have known. She must have come here."

At the center of the chamber stood a low pedestal of carved marble. Resting upon it was a lyre wrought in gold, strings gleaming though no hand touched them.

The air quivered with faint notes, unstruck, yet present, like the echo of a song waiting to be born.

Ella stepped forward slowly. The golden sparks that so often flickered around her journal now shimmered across the chamber, drifting upward like fireflies to gather near the lyre.

Her heart pounded. "It feels like another world."

She reached out but stopped short of touching the lyre. The air around it vibrated gently, humming against her palm as though greeting her.

Betty June came beside her, laying a hand on her shoulder. "This is no curse, Ella. This is legacy. Your mother wanted you to see this, but only when you were old enough and ready."

Ella closed her eyes, and for a moment, she swore she heard her mother's voice, faint but clear, carry it with love, not fear.

Tears welled as she opened her eyes again. The angels on the walls seemed to glow brighter, their painted faces filled with quiet joy.

She turned to Caleb, whispering, "Do you feel it?"

His eyes were wide, reflecting the golden light. "I feel you and your joy and peace," he said softly. "And that's enough."

The chamber's glow dimmed slightly, settling back into quiet radiance, as though content to wait. Glitterella drew back her hand, her breath trembling.

"We'll return," she said, her voice steadier than she felt. "When the letter opens. When it's time."

Betty June nodded. "Yes. This place has waited this long. It can wait a little longer."

Together, they climbed the stairs, leaving the chamber bathed in its heavenly glow. But as the door closed behind them, Ella knew she had only glimpsed the beginning.

Antonín's fury was quiet, the kind that chilled more than shouts. He stood in the library when they returned, his hands gripping the back of a chair, knuckles white.

"You went below," he said without turning.

Glitterella swallowed. Caleb shifted closer, his steady presence bracing her. "Yes. We found it."

At that, Antonín spun. His eyes burned, not only with anger but with fear. "That chamber is not a place to wander into like curious children. It holds power none of us fully commands. That is why your mother sealed it away. That is why I told you to wait!"

Betty June stepped forward, her voice even but firm. "She was called to it, Antonín. Can't you see? The castle itself responded. You can no more keep her from it than you can keep the sun from rising."

Glitterella's voice trembled but held. "I don't think it meant to harm me. It felt… holy. Like a blessing, not a curse."

His jaw tightened. "You only saw the surface. The letter will tell you more. Wait until then."

The days that followed pressed with heavy expectation. Her birthday crept closer, each hour thick with waiting. Servants polished the halls, candles were set in every sconce, as though the entire castle was prepared not for a celebration, it seemed, but for a revelation.

At last, the morning arrived. Antonín stood solemnly by the hearth. Aunt Betty June rested a hand on Glitterella's shoulder. Calebs seated close to her.

With trembling fingers, Glitterella broke the seal.

Inside, the writing was her mother's.

Dearest Ella,

If you are reading this, then you have found the chamber of angels. I prayed you would reach it when your heart was ready. It is not a tomb, but a sanctuary. It will answer your songs' messages and meanings and magnify them, but only if your heart is true. Carry it with love, not fear, and it will never consume you.

There is more. Beneath the murals lies another door, hidden behind the shelf of psalms. There you will find a small box. It is not much, but it is yours. What is inside will remind you of who you are, and who you were always meant to become.

This is my last gift to you, Ella. Not the castle, not the legacy, but the piece of my heart I could not take with me. May it guide you when shadows rise.

Always with you my lovely daughter,
Mother

Tears blurred her vision as she lowered the letter. Aunt Betty June wiped her eyes quietly. Caleb kissed her temple, whispering, "If you are ready... let's go."

Back in the chamber, the golden glow rose higher, as if welcoming her return. The painted angels seemed to shine even brighter. Guided by her mother's words, she pressed her hand against the carved shelf of psalms. With a push, the shelf turned inward, revealing a narrow alcove. There, upon a stone ledge, rested a small velvet-lined box.

Her hands trembled as she lifted it. She opened it slowly. Inside lay a heart-shaped locket of gold on a golden chain, its face engraved with a single star. When she touched it, the golden sparks flared to life, swirling around her like a living flame.

She gasped. The locket grew warm, and for an instant, she felt her mother's presence so vividly she thought she might faint. A whisper touched her heart, tender and certain: I am with you still.

Ella clutched it to her heart, tears streaming freely. Caleb's arms closed around her, Aunt Betty June's hand rested on her back, and even Antonín, silent in the doorway, bowed his head.

The chamber seemed to hum, a soft chord rising as though the angels themselves rejoiced.

This was no curse. This was love, sealed in gold, passed from mother to daughter.

And now, it was hers.

That evening, the locket rested on the bedside table, its golden star catching and scattering the candlelight as though it already carried a fire of its own. Glitterella sat on the edge of the bed, her hands clasped tightly in her lap, unable to tear her gaze away. Caleb tuned the Stauffer softly, the warm notes filling the chamber like a heartbeat. His voice was gentle. "You don't have to be afraid of it, Ella. It's meant for you."

His words loosened something in her chest. With trembling fingers, she reached for it. The gold heart was cool as it slid against her skin, but the moment the clasp of the chain clicked into place, a warmth pulsed through her as steady as breath. It was not sharp or frightening, only insistent, like a second heartbeat rising to meet her own.

She pressed the pendant against her chest. A tear slipped free. "It feels… alive."

Later that evening, they went down to the library. Aunt Betty June, seated near the fire with her scarf drawn close, leaned forward. "Your mother wore that locket every day until she could no longer sing. She told me it wasn't jewelry; it was magical and a promise."

Glitterella's eyebrows raised. She touched the pendant lightly, as though the gold might answer her.

Caleb strummed a chord, low, inviting. The sound lingered, filling the space between them. He gave her a small nod. "Sing with me."

Her journal lay across her knees. She opened it, though the words inside seemed unnecessary now. The melody rose from her, tentative at first, then stronger, her voice weaving with the chords Caleb played.

At once, the sparks came. Not faint, not flickering, they poured from the pages in golden ribbons, curling upward, wrapping around her arms, spiraling toward the locket. The pendant flared, light spilling across the room.

Aunt Betty June gasped. Caleb's strumming faltered as he stared, wonder widening his eyes.

CHAPTER THIRTY-ONE
A Voice That Cannot Be Silenced

A new invitation had arrived, gilded and heavily, sealed with a deep crimson wax. Another castle, not far across the valley, was hosting a winter ball. Dignitaries, musicians, and patrons from Vienna would be there. Antonín insisted it was time Glitterella be seen, not as a guest, but as Celestýn's heir.

The night of the ball, the halls of Château Kavanagh glittered with chandeliers, their crystals scattering light like stars. The air was warm with wine and perfume, gowns swirled across the marble floors, and music rippled from a string quartet.

Glitterella stood at Caleb's side, her gown pale blue satin, the gold locket gleaming. He carried the Stauffer guitar in its polished case, his black tuxedo fitting him like it had been made for him alone. She felt the warmth of his hand brushing hers as they were led to the small stage set near the grand staircase.

Antonín's voice had been firm earlier: "You will not hide your gift. Tonight, you let the world see."

Her pulse raced. She touched the locket for steadiness. Caleb leaned close, whispering, "It's just us, Ella, relax!"

The room hushed as they began. Caleb's fingers danced across the guitar strings, a low, rich prelude. Glitterella's voice rose to join him, tentative at first, then soaring, her notes threading with his chords.

The locket warmed instantly. Sparks shimmered faintly at the edges of her vision, not wild and unrestrained, but soft, like golden dust scattering in the air. The audience leaned forward, breath held, their glasses stilled midair, toasting to the beautiful music.

As the song built, the sparks grew brighter, weaving between her and Caleb. She caught his gaze, his eyes wide with awe, though his playing never faltered. Together, their music rose, entwined, two voices becoming one flame.

A woman in the front pressed a hand to her heart.

A man wiped his eyes, startled by the depth of his own emotion. The locket pulsed with each note, steady as a heartbeat, guiding Ella's voice higher, richer, freer.

When the final refrain came, soft and tender, she and Caleb sang it together:

Heart to heart, our song will stay,
Guiding us home, come what may.
Every note, forever true,
Our music lives in us and you.

The room fell silent as the last chord faded, golden sparks curling around them before dissolving into the vaulted air. For a heartbeat, nothing stirred.

Then thunderous applause erupted. The audience rose to their feet, clapping, cheering, some even weeping openly.

Glitterella's breath shook, her gaze darting to Caleb. His smile was small but fierce, pride and love blazing in his eyes.

She touched the locket as the applause washed over them. For the first time, she felt no fear of its glow. It was not a burden, not a curse. It was her mother's gift, and tonight, it had become theirs.

Later, as they slipped into a quiet antechamber, Caleb leaned in close, his hand still trembling from the strings. "Did you feel it? The way the sparks followed the song. It was like the whole room was inside the music with us."

Ella nodded, her voice soft. "It wasn't just all of us. It was her too. My mother." She touched the locket, her eyes glistening. "And maybe more than her. Maybe every Celestýn who ever carried this."

Caleb kissed her, whispering, "Then tonight wasn't just a performance. It was a promise. You and me, whatever this legacy asks, we'll face it together."

Outside, the applause still thundered through the marble halls. Inside, in the hush of their shared moment, Glitterella knew: her gift was no longer hidden, her legacy no longer a secret.

The world had begun to see.

The applause followed them off the stage, echoing through the vaulted hall like a tide that would not recede. Guests crowded near, their faces bright with awe and flushed with wine.

"Magnificent," one noblewoman whispered, clutching her pearls. "I've never heard such purity of voice."

"Not voice alone," a composer murmured, his sharp eyes fixed on Glitterella. "The air itself seemed to move. Did you feel it?"

Others pressed closer, showering her with questions: where had she trained, what master had taught her, what secrets of technique she possessed. Ella smiled politely, but her pulse raced. No master had taught her what had just happened. No lesson could explain the golden sparks that had wrapped themselves around the music.

A young baron leaned toward Caleb, admiration glinting in his gaze. "You play with fire, sir, yet somehow she carries it without burning."

From across the room, Ella noticed a pair of older men in quiet conversation, their expressions wary. She caught only fragments: Celestýn… dangerous… the gift returns. A chill rippled through her. Not everyone saw wonder in the sparks; some saw threat.

At last, Antonín appeared, his presence cutting through the crowd. His voice was firm but calm. "Lady Celestýn requires rest." With a subtle gesture, he cleared a path through the throng. Caleb guided Glitterella at his side, and Aunt Betty June followed closely.

They retreated into a smaller chamber, the noise of the ballroom muffled by heavy doors. Here, only the crackle of a fire and the clink of glasses from a nearby sideboard remained.

Antonín studied her, his expression unreadable. "You did not hide it. Good. The world must know who you are."

Betty June frowned. "But did you see their faces, Antonín? Not all of them applauded. Some were afraid. Some will twist this."

"Let them," he said coldly. "Let them have their doubts. Eventually, they will all believe."

Caleb spoke before Antonín could reply. "Tonight wasn't about power; it was about love. And anyone who saw it clearly knows the difference."

Antonín's gaze flicked between them, his lips pressed thin. Finally, he exhaled, slow and heavy. "Yes, but remember, every gift draws both reverence and envy. That is the burden of the Celestýn name."

Betty June touched Ella's shoulder gently. "And it is also its blessing. Tonight, you gave them beauty. Whatever shadows linger, don't forget the light."

Ella looked at the locket, still warm against her skin. She thought of the crowd's wonder, the whispers in the corner. She thought of Caleb's voice threading into hers, steady and true.

Her heart steadied. "Then I will sing for the light. Always."

Caleb's hand found hers, "And I'll be there, with you always and for every note."

For a moment, silence wrapped around them, not empty, but full, like the pause before the first note of a new song.

Outside, the music of the ball swelled again. Inside, Glitterella knew this: the world had seen her, truly seen her, and nothing could return her to the shadows.

As they were leaving the ball, an older carriage had been taken out, and its wheels were scarcely cooled in the courtyard when Antonín stumbled against it. He had walked tall all night, his bearing unbent even in age, but now, as snow dusted the steps, his cane slipped, his breath caught, and he fell.

"Uncle!" Glitterella cried, dropping beside him, her gown pooling in the snow. Caleb was at her side in an instant, lifting Antonín's shoulders. Aunt Betty June knelt opposite, her hands trembling as she tried to find his pulse.

"Send for the physician!" Caleb ran into the castle, and his voice rang down the hall as servants rushed forward.

But Antonín's eyes had already dulled. His lips moved faintly, forming words that Glitterella strained to hear. She bent close, tears stinging her eyes.

"You… are the legacy now," he whispered. "Carry it with love… not fear."

And then his hand slackened in hers.

The world stilled. The courtyard, the wind, even the falling snow seemed to hush as though the castle itself bowed its head.

Aunt Betty June pressed a hand to her mouth. Caleb closed his eyes with grief. Glitterella clutched Antonín's still hand, sobbing softly, "No, not yet… I just found you. Please."

But he was gone. By the time they carried him inside, the news had spread through the household. Servants lined the great hall, some weeping quietly, others bowing their heads in silence.

When the morning of the funeral arrived, the air was sharp and cold. Bells echoed over the hills as Glitterella walked the corridor beside Aunt Betty June. Neither spoke. The scent of roses and wax lingered like a memory.

The chapel was full. Servants stood along the walls in black, heads bowed. Caleb waited near the front, his expression drawn but calm.

Antonín lay still in his casket, framed by white flowers and a dark velvet cloth embroidered with the family crest. The stained glass above him spilled color across his face, reds, blues, and golds that seemed to breathe life back into the quiet.

The priest spoke about legacy, love, and the courage to leave something behind. Glitterella barely heard. Still in shock…

After the service, they followed the casket outside. Snow fell again, soft and seemingly endless. Glitterella laid a single white rose on the top. Aunt Betty June's arm slipped around her waist as Caleb stood on her other side, silent but steady.

Back inside the castle, it now felt a bit hollow, every sound a little too loud. Fires burned in the hearths, but the warmth didn't reach very far. The staff waited in the great hall, their grief quiet but visible.

Then one of the stewards stepped forward. His voice was gentle, but the way he held himself made everyone still. "My lady," he said gently, with a kind of reverence. toward Glitterella. "He left this in my care, with strict instructions."

He handed her an envelope sealed with black wax, the Celestýn crest pressed deep into the surface.

Glitterella turned it over in her hands. The paper was heavy, faintly warm from the steward's touch. "He said you'd know when to open it," the man added softly.

Aunt Betty June stood beside her, eyes glistening. "Whatever it is, darling, it's yours now."

Glitterella looked down at the seal, her pulse tapping at her wrist. She just held it close and whispered, almost to herself, "Then I'll carry it with love. Just like he told me to." Her fingers trembled as she broke the seal. The letter was brief, written in Antonín's firm hand:

To my niece, Celestýn, called Glitterella,
I leave the castle, the lands, and all titles of our line. To
her, and to the music that binds her, I entrust what I
could no longer carry. May she do what I could not: turn
burden into blessing, and fear into peace and light.

Glitterella's tears fell freely onto the parchment. She
looked up, her vision blurred, to find every eye upon her,
the staff, Aunt Betty June, Caleb steady at her side.

"I don't know if I can do this," she whispered.

Caleb slipped his hand into hers, his voice firm.

"My love, I am here always. We'll do it together."

Betty June crossed the room, her scarf trailing
behind her like a shadow of the past. She placed a hand
on Ella's shoulder. "Your mother trusted me to keep you
safe. Antonín trusted you to lead. But love, Ella, the real
and pure love you have within, this kind of love will be
what makes you worthy of it."

The steward bowed low. "Lady Celestýn, the house
is yours. We are yours."

Around the hall, servants bent their heads in unison.
The flickering candles seemed to flare brighter, as if the
castle itself acknowledged the vow.

Glitterella clutched the locket against her skin. Its
warmth pulsed once, steady and sure. Golden sparks
stirred faintly in the rafters, swirling down like stardust.
The household gasped, some crossing themselves, others
weeping at the sight.

Ella lifted her chin through her tears, her voice
steady though soft. "Then hear me. I will not rule with
fear. I will not carry this alone. This house, this legacy, it
will be built on truth, on courage, and on love. Always
love."

The sparks brightened, curling around her like a crown of light. Caleb's hand steadied hers. Betty June's eyes shone with pride and sorrow.

And for the first time since her mother's passing, Glitterella felt the weight of her inheritance not as a shackle, but as a blessing and a promise, binding her to everyone gathered, and to the generations before.

The Celestýn legacy was no longer hidden. It lived now in her, in them, in all who would walk with her into the days to come.

Caleb was the first to break the silence. His voice was reverent, steady. "Your gift isn't just yours, it's hers too. Your mother's spirit is still with you, through every note."

Ella clutched the locket, sobs shaking her shoulders.

"I thought I'd lost her. But she never left."

Aunt Betty June rose and came to her. Her voice cracked. "She poured herself into you, Ella, into this. She wanted you to have what she could not. You're her song continued."

Caleb placed his guitar aside and drew Ella gently against him, her head pressed to his chest. He whispered into her hair, steady and certain, "You'll never have to carry it alone. Not while I'm here."

The fire crackled, filling the silence. For the first time, the castle felt less like a cage of secrets and more like a sanctuary, an ancient heart opening to let them in.

Glitterella touched the locket. She understood now: it was not only her mother's farewell. It was her mother's presence, her promise, her light.

And with Caleb's arm around her, Betty June's hand still holding hers, and Antonín's vow settling into the air, she knew this truth: she was not alone.

Aunt Betty June stood near the front, her eyes watchful but encouraging. As Ella stepped forward, the murmur of the servants hushed. She felt Caleb's steady presence beside her, grounding her, his hand brushing hers in silent strength.

She began, her voice wavering at first but then finding its strength. "I am so sad that we lost Lord Antonín. A leader, a protector, and, though I had so little time to know him, my uncle. I grieve with you."

A ripple of nods passed through the hall.

She lifted her chin, the locket glinting in the candlelight. "But he has left us not in shadow, but in trust. He entrusted this house, this legacy, to me. To us. I cannot carry it alone. I will not. This place will not be ruled by fear or secrecy, but by truth, by courage, and by love. Always love."

As the words left her, the golden sparks stirred again. They shimmered faintly above the assembly, cascading like stardust before fading into the air. Gasps broke the silence; some bowed their heads; others pressed their hands to their hearts.

Aunt Betty June's eyes shone with tears. Caleb's gaze never left her, pride and devotion etched into every line of his face. The steward bowed deeply. "Lady Celestýn, we are yours." For the first time, she wasn't only Glitterella, the girl who sang in borrowed light. She was Celestýn, heir of a legacy, keeper of its gift, and leader of those who now looked to her. And with Caleb at her side, she knew she would not falter.

CHAPTER THIRTY-TWO
The Ring of Starlight

At the tall window of her chamber, Glitterella stood quiet, her reflection blurred in the frost. Below, the courtyard lay blanketed in perfectly fallen snow, each drift touched by moonlight, each tower wrapped in silence. The locket at her throat felt warm, alive, as if keeping the faintest heartbeat of the past.

The days after Antonín's passing unfolded in a rhythm all their own, grief giving way to quiet resolve, silence shaping itself into a new song. The castle mourned, yet beneath the sorrow, something gentle stirred: a pulse of renewal, of light rediscovering its path through shadow. Celestýn Castle had not fallen into darkness. It was only waiting for her to become what she was always meant to be.

She walked the corridors that once carried Antonín's footsteps, tracing the smooth curve of the banister burnished by time. Every echo seemed to whisper his guidance; every candle flicker breathed his memory. Servants murmured her new name with reverence, Lady Celestýn, but to her it felt like a melody she had yet to learn, soft and unfinished.

Letters began to arrive from Prague and Vienna, some bound in black ribbon, others gilded in gold. Condolences, invitations, requests. The world beyond these walls still turned, but her heart remained tethered here, in the space between endings and beginnings.

That quiet evening, as snow melted into glassy frost along the parapets, Caleb appeared at her door with a smile. His voice carried gentleness, but beneath it she heard the steady rhythm of intent.

"Come with me," he said, offering his hand.

She let him help her into her coat, his touch lingering long enough to stir the air between them. Together they descended the grand staircase, their steps echoing softly through the great hall. Outside, lanterns swayed from the arches, their glow breathing against the twilight. The gardens shimmered under the stars, each branch dusted with frost, each petal etched in silver.

They walked in silence at first, their fingers interlaced, their pace unhurried, until he stopped beneath the old marble archway where the frozen fountain gleamed like glass. Frost clung to the statues, and moonlight pooled around them like water reborn.

"Do you remember," he said quietly, "when you sang on the bridge in Prague? The lanterns, the river, your voice carried so far, I thought the stars would bend to listen. I knew then that nothing could ever be more beautiful."

Her lips curved faintly. "And yet you stayed to prove me wrong?"

He smiled, that calm, knowing smile she loved. "I stayed because I already knew. Wherever you are, that's home. Not Vienna. Not Prague. You, I love you Glitterella, with all my heart and soul."

The world seemed to still as he dropped to one knee. Snow whispered beneath him, soft as silk. From his coat pocket, he drew a small velvet box, the hinge catching the light as if time itself had paused to watch.

He opened it, revealing a ring unlike any she had ever seen. At its crown rested a sapphire shaped like a star, its depth the color of midnight seas, shot through with veins of rose and blue fire. Diamonds cascaded around it in a halo of soft brilliance, shimmering like starlight caught in motion.

Caleb's voice trembled before steadying.

"It's called the Starlight Stone. When Antonín gave it to me, he told me it was once part of the Celestýn crown. When the castle fell silent generations ago, it vanished until now. He said it would return only when love found its way back to this house, and it should be yours forever."

He drew a breath. "Glitterella Celestýn," he whispered, the words trembling between them...

"Will you marry me?"

Her surprised laughter broke through her joyful tears, a sound bright and real as bells in spring. "Yes," she said, her voice catching with joy. "Yes, oh... a thousand times yes."

When he rose from his knee, she fell into his arms, and the locket between them glowed. Its light mingled with the sapphire's fire until both pulsed together, their warmth breathing life into the cold night. Golden sparks drifted upward, swirling like blessings made visible, scattering across the air like newborn stars.

Above the towers of Celestýn Castle, the bells tolled once more, deep, resonant, alive. No longer for mourning. For love reborn.

Later that night, Glitterella stood on the balcony alone, the ring gleaming on her hand. The moonlight gathered on its facets, spilling over her fingers in rivers of blue and silver. She turned her hand with the sapphire ring slowly, watching how it would sparkle with its own glimmering light, as though it still remembered the crown it once adorned.

The Starlight Ring. The legacy reborn through her.

Her breath rose in faint clouds, dissolving into the cold air. She leaned forward, the stars burned bright and clear, alive with promise.

Somewhere in the stillness, a sound drifted upward. A single note, so tender, threading through the hush like silk through twilight. She stilled, listening. Caleb's melody. His guitar was the perfect sound to close this wonderful evening as the notes he played floated from the great hall below, soft at first, then swelling with quiet strength.

The music rose and curved around her, finding her where the night met the wind. She closed her eyes, letting it wash through her, the memory of their song, the echo of all they had lost and found again. Every chord seemed to breathe her name.

The sapphire and the locket flickered faintly, like a pulse in rhythm with the music. For an instant, the whole world felt suspended, poised between what had been and what might come.

She whispered into the night, voice trembling but sure, "This isn't the end."

The melody answered, low and steady.

She smiled through the shimmer of her tears, the ring catching the first pale light of dawn.

The story wasn't ending.

It was beginning again.

ABOUT THE AUTHOR

Tricia Greenwood is an author, songwriter, and music producer whose stories and songs intertwine like notes in a single melody. Through her publishing imprint, HeartSpeak Publishing, and her music label, HeartSpeak Music, she creates books and albums that celebrate love, imagination, and the power of dreams.

Her writing brings to life worlds where music is more than sound; it is courage, connection, and truth. From whimsical adventures for children to heartfelt ballads and novels of self-discovery, Tricia's work is devoted to the belief that creativity can heal, inspire, and remind us of who we are.

With every page she writes and every song she sings, Tricia carries one mission forward: to touch hearts.

A Message from Tricia

Thank you for taking the time to spend with *Glitterella*.

Though she was born from my imagination, the feelings she carries are real, ones I've known, too.

I created Glitterella as a reminder that sparkle isn't only about glitter or bright lights. It's about finding the courage to step forward when you'd rather stay hidden. It's about speaking the truth, even when your voice trembles. It's about choosing kindness when it isn't easy and holding fast to a dream when letting go would seem simpler.

So here is my wish for you:

Write the song. Tell your story. Begin the project that has been waiting for your hands. Dance barefoot in your kitchen. Sing like no one is listening.

And never forget, the sparkle you've been searching for has always been within you, waiting to shine.

With love,

Tricia Greenwood

Download

Glitterella's Songs

Scan the QR code below for Glitterella's new album...

🎵 *Let It Shine*
🎵 *The Light Inside of Me*

These songs and more are available now at
HeartSpeakmusic.com
Because light grows brighter when we sing it together.
🤍

📱 **Scan the QR code to start listening!**

And more...
Also, full-color pictures of Glitterella
And As A Young Girl You can see her in
Childrens books here:
www.TheKindnessClubForKids.com